She smiled, and all the s... Lauren he'd taken in his head over the last few days were highlighted by that smile.

And he was—

What?

Smitten?

Good grief!

That was far too strong a word.

Maybe it was just fascination—she was so unlike any woman he'd ever known.

And beautiful.

Maybe it was just lust, although he didn't think lust would have him waiting, almost breathless, for a smile.

Or wanting to hear her voice, no matter the topic, speaking quietly just to him.

And surely it had to be more than lust, when the teasing glint in her eyes could leave him mute.

He knew for sure whatever this was, it had never happened to him before, not with girlfriends, or Maddie's mother—anyone, in fact. Yet here he was, walking one step behind her, wanting to reach out and clasp her hips. Or walk alongside her so he could sling an arm casually around her waist, then, as their pace slowed, turn her to him and kiss her in the night-scented bush.

Dear Reader,

Some books seem to come together neatly and easily while others get lost along the way. This book was one of the latter mainly because my mind kept wandering off on tangents, which meant the love story I was supposed to be writing suffered.

What a lot of readers probably don't realize is that without editors very few books would get to a publishable stage. As writers we whine and moan about editors and revisions, but it is thanks to our editors—and in this case, thanks to my editor— that we finally pull our books into the kind of story our readers will enjoy.

Over the course of my career as a writer, I have been blessed with many excellent editors who have managed to hammer my stories into the best possible shape, making them stories I can be proud of. So a big thank-you to all of them, and in particular my current editor, who refused to let me abandon this book!

Meredith

A WEDDING FOR THE SINGLE DAD

MEREDITH WEBBER

HARLEQUIN
MEDICAL
ROMANCE

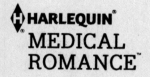

HARLEQUIN®
MEDICAL
ROMANCE™

Recycling programs
for this product may
not exist in your area.

ISBN-13: 978-1-335-40438-1

A Wedding for the Single Dad

Copyright © 2021 by Meredith Webber

This edition published by arrangement with Harlequin Books S.A.

For questions and comments about the quality of this book, please contact us at CustomerService@Harlequin.com.

Harlequin Enterprises ULC
22 Adelaide St. West, 40th Floor
Toronto, Ontario M5H 4E3, Canada
www.Harlequin.com

Printed in U.S.A.

Meredith Webber lives on the sunny Gold Coast in Queensland, Australia, but takes regular trips west into the outback, fossicking for gold or opal. These breaks in the beautiful and sometimes cruel red-earth country provide her with an escape from the writing desk and a chance for her mind to roam free—not to mention getting some much-needed exercise. They also supply the kernels of so many stories that it's hard for her to stop writing!

Books by Meredith Webber

Harlequin Medical Romance

Bondi Bay Heroes

Healed by Her Army Doc

The Halliday Family

A Forever Family for the Army Doc
Engaged to the Doctor Sheikh
A Miracle for the Baby Doctor
From Bachelor to Daddy

New Year Wedding for the Crown Prince
A Wife for the Surgeon Sheikh
The Doctors' Christmas Reunion
Conveniently Wed in Paradise
One Night to Forever Family

Visit the Author Profile page
at Harlequin.com for more titles.

CHAPTER ONE

'WHO THE HELL are you?'

'Says the man lying in a creek bed and lucky to be alive! Shoulder bad? Possibly dislocated, from the look of things,' Lauren said, hoping she sounded cooler and more in command than she felt. There'd been something about the very English male voice that had made the demand sound more abrupt than it might otherwise have.

Something about it, too, that had skittered down her spine.

She'd come expecting injury, but not an enormous man—at least six foot two or three—with night-dark tousled hair and a chippy attitude.

She smiled at him to cover her own uncertainty—she just didn't do skittery spines.

'I'm your friendly neighbourhood rescuer, Lauren Henderson, although what you were doing flitting around up there in Henry's home-made flying machine I can't imagine.'

She'd drawn closer to the man by now, and

he didn't look any smaller. From his snapped retort—'It's an ultralight!'—it was clear he also wasn't any happier.

'Which doesn't answer the question, but I guess I'd better have a look at you. There's a team trudging up the path somewhere behind me, but even on a stretcher you'll be more comfortable if I get your shoulder back into place before they carry you down.'

A grumbling noise suggested that he might argue about being carried down the gully, but really he had no choice.

She approached him fairly tentatively, and not only partly because of the rocky terrain—the dangers of wounded wild beasts were featuring in the forefront of her imagination...

There was no sign of blood, which didn't rule out the possibility that he wasn't lying in a puddle of it, and his eyes—an unusual dark blue— were alert.

Too alert?

'Apart from your shoulder, are you in pain?' she asked, easing her backpack off her shoulders and setting it to one side as she knelt beside him.

'I fell out of the sky! Of course, I'm in pain. Ouch!'

Lauren had been feeling around his head as he muttered at her, and touching the slight lump on the back of his skull had caused the 'ouch'.

'Can you move your legs and your good arm?' she asked, and although he groaned as he did it the three limbs moved fairly normally.

'Well, let's get your shoulder sorted,' she said, 'before the others get here.'

'What do you mean—get it sorted?'

The man was in pain, so she bit back a smart retort.

'Pop it back into place. You'll still need to be carried out and have it X-rayed when you get to civilisation, because there will be damage to the cartilage and tendons.'

She'd removed 'the magic green whistle', as football players called the handy device, while she was speaking, and now passed it to him. 'Take about six breaths,' she said.

Dark blue eyes narrowed suspiciously. 'What's in it?' he asked.

'Methoxyfluorane,' she said calmly, getting herself into position beside his left shoulder, prepared to lift his arm whether it hurt him or not. But the man was in a lot of pain—she had to grant him a little leeway...

Also, he was very intriguing *and* very attractive. And quite possibly—probably—her new neighbour. Henry's nephew or great-nephew, she seemed to remember...

She watched him breathe in the pain-relief

drug and hid a smile as it obviously started to work, relaxing the tension in his body.

'Now, I'm just going to bend your arm at the elbow and move it like this, and with a bit of pressure I should be able to slip it back into place.'

'Are you a qualified paramedic? Should you be doing this?'

Okay, so methoxyfluorane hadn't improved his mood. But he *had* crashed down from the sky, and he was probably feeling extremely foolish for having attempted to fly the ultralight, as well as being in a great deal of pain.

So she smiled sweetly at him.

'No and yes,' she said, and before he could voice further objections she lifted his folded arm and moved it upward and outward until she felt the joint slip back into its socket.

'Better?' she said, although she knew it would still be painful—just not agonisingly so.

He muttered something she was charitably willing to accept as assent, and she began to examine the rest of him. Bloody graze on his left hand—he'd probably put it out to break his fall—and his left ankle looked a little swollen.

'Sore?' she asked, moving it slightly.

More muttered complaints followed as she unlaced his light canvas shoes.

'I'm going to take off your shoe and sock so I

can bandage it,' she told him. 'If we leave them on and your ankle swells, your shoe will have to be cut off—which would be a pity with such good-quality footwear.'

More mutterings. This time she gathered something about what a woman would know about men's footwear. She ignored the words and went ahead, removing his shoe, and then his sock, revealing a long, pale foot, with blue veins visible beneath milky skin.

The bare foot made him seem vulnerable, and for all his tetchy remarks she suddenly felt sorry for him.

Which, she decided, was distinctly better than the physical reaction she'd had earlier…

She'd just finished binding the ankle when voices told her the SES team had arrived.

'He okay?' the lead man asked.

Lauren nodded. 'I've just reset a dislocated left shoulder—it'll need to be X-rayed—and checked him over for other injuries. His left arm will need to be put into a special sling for a while, and his left ankle…'

But the team were no longer listening.

'Geez,' one of them said, peering up at the tangle of fine wood and plastic in the midst of the dead black trees that bordered the gully. 'Is that old Henry's flying machine up there? Boy, he'll be cranky up in heaven!'

'Or down in hell,' another suggested, and all four laughed before slowly returning their attention to their patient.

'You did that?' they more or less chorused, all shaking their heads in disbelief.

'Okay,' Lauren said, calling them to order as they started to suggest the punishments old Henry would have meted out to someone crashing his most favourite toy. 'You've actually got a patient here, and if you want to get him down the track in daylight I'd suggest you get him strapped onto whatever you're carrying and start moving.'

'I don't need to be carried.'

Not muttered, but definitely not happy.

'You might have other injuries, and possibly concussion,' she told him, adding firmly, 'So you *will* be carried.'

Recalled to their job, the team set to work, and as they slid the pieces of stretcher under the injured man Lauren could practically read their minds.

Although in case she'd been in any doubt Joe, their leader, muttered, 'Cor, he's a big bugger!'

'I'll take the head end and you can go two each side,' she said. 'The ambulance will be down on the road. You can radio for their two guys to start up the track to help.'

They worked well, the team, getting the bits

of board under the patient and snapped together, strapping him firmly onto it.

'Just use the magic whistle if you need to,' Lauren reminded the man, as they all got into position to lift him.

He gave her a look of such disbelief she had to smile.

'They *have* done it before,' she said, and he shut his eyes, as if better to pretend this wasn't happening.

He'd been rescued by—he couldn't think off-hand of a bunch of comedians to compare this lot to—vaudeville slapstick clowns, perhaps?

Campbell Grahame shook his head—big mistake, as it brought the sore lump on it into contact with the board to which he'd been strapped. He clutched the device his rescuer had called 'the magic whistle' to his chest, wondering if he should take a few more puffs as the lurching downhill journey was anything but comfortable.

His rescuer!

Maybe he'd think about *her* instead of the pain.

She'd seemed to appear from nowhere, startling him as he'd tried to work out just how seriously he was injured. *And* told himself how stupid he'd been! He'd been angry with himself, as well, for flying so far in an old machine he didn't know at all. Apart from anything else, it had been totally irresponsible.

He turned his attention back to his rescuer.

Totally unsympathetic, she'd been, whoever she was. But perhaps brisk efficiency was what was needed in rescue situations.

Still, a rescuer with long, tanned legs, clad in short red shorts and a singlet that clung to a curvy upper body like a second skin...? The men at least were in uniform—with the words State Emergency Service embroidered on their shirts.

The peaked black cap she was wearing, pulled down tightly on her forehead, meant he hadn't been able to see the hair tucked under it, but dark eyes and eyebrows suggested it would be brown or black.

He raised his eyes to take another look at her face, hoping she was concentrating on where she was putting her feet rather than on him.

But it was a surreptitious glance, just to check that her face was as lovely as he remembered it.

It was.

It was well put together, with a straight nose and wide, shapely lips, a small, determined chin—yes, she was something of a beauty... although he did wonder if other people would think so.

Perhaps it was just a face like any other, and

he'd imbued it with beauty because she'd rescued him?

Whatever. The fact remained he'd been damnably rude to her.

He sighed, and the beauty—he was pretty sure she *was* a beauty—said, 'Don't be afraid to use the whistle. This isn't exactly the smoothest ride you'll ever have, and there could be other things wrong with you.'

But he knew there weren't. The team had carried out the basic tests—blood pressure, heart-rate, breathing—and although he felt pain as they trekked down the rough track, he knew it wasn't anything serious.

So he could think about the woman again—tall, as well as good looking...

'What's your name?'

His question came out without much forethought, and she frowned down at him, as if she wasn't certain of the answer.

Had she already told him?

He couldn't remember...

'Lauren Henderson,' she said eventually, before adding, 'And yours?'

Cam frowned. He *had* introduced himself earlier—but had that been just to the team?

Surely she'd heard?

'Campbell Grahame—I'm usually called Cam.'

One of the two men who held the stretcher

at Cam's shoulder level turned briefly towards them, but a slight slip on a rock had him turning back, concentrating on where he was going, almost immediately.

'How do you do, Cam?' Lauren said, in the slightly husky voice that somehow suited her. 'I won't shake hands because I'd probably drop you.' Silent for a moment, she then said, 'And what *were* you up to—flying over the forest in old Henry's ancient machine?'

All four of the heads he could see in front of him turned at this question, and he wondered if perhaps they should leave conversation until they were well away from the rough track by the creek bed.

But she *had* asked…

'I thought it might be useful to spot any injured wildlife returning to their burnt-out homes.'

'You've never heard of drones?' It was a question edged with sarcasm, but perhaps—

'Is that why I crashed? You had a drone up and it hit me?'

She gave a huff of laughter and shook her head. 'You crashed because you were flying so low your left wing-tip hit a tree, and you were lucky I did have a drone up—because otherwise it would have taken a full-scale search, and almost certainly plenty of man hours, to find you. The forest might be burnt out, but there's thick regeneration in the undergrowth, and with the deep gullies even a helicopter search would have been difficult, if not impossible.'

'Well, that's telling me,' he muttered to himself, feeling put out that he wasn't being treated more kindly, considering he was injured. Not that he'd earned any kindness, the way he'd been earlier—though his bad temper was more to do with his own foolishness than these innocent rescuers.

They continued down the path in silence, and as the journey went on he realised just how far this group had walked to rescue him—idiot that he was to have even got into the damn microlight.

'Do you do this often?' he asked.

'Rescue blokes from crashed flying machines?' one of the men responded. 'Not so much. But I reckon a couple of dozen times a summer we get call-outs to search for someone who hasn't come back when they should...a fisherman stranded on rocks in the lake as the tide rises, lost bush-walkers, kids—we keep busy.'

Intrigued now, Cam wanted to know more. 'Only in summer?'

Another of the men shook his head. 'Nah! Winter's actually worse—cooler for people who want to walk some of the trails though the bush, who then get off the trail and end up lost.'

'Not that there'll be much bush to walk in this year,' another said, gloom shrouding his words.

And then the talk turned to the bushfires that had so recently ravaged the area. Most of South Eastern Australia had suffered to some degree, and Cam, who'd arrived in the country six days ago, in the aftermath of the fires, had discovered that as well as inheriting a veterinary practice from a great-uncle he'd only met once, many years earlier, he'd inherited a small hospital for injured wildlife—complete with, and run by, mostly volunteer helpers.

And an ultralight!

He bit back a groan, more of anguish than agony. Flying the wretched machine had seemed like a challenge. And it had brought back such vivid memories!

The only time he'd met his great-uncle, Henry had helped him build his very own ultralight, and taught him how to fly it. So, seeing what must have been Henry's old machine in the shed, it had been hard to resist—particularly as his daughter had been so excited that Daddy could fly such a thing.

Showing off to Maddie. How pathetic had that been?

Idiotic too.

Maddie!

Hell!

He looked up at rescuer number one. 'Can someone radio the vet surgery and let my mother know I'm okay? She'll be worried.'

'I'll do it,' one of the men at the foot of the stretcher said, keeping hold of his burden with one hand, while the other tapped away at a radio Velcroed to his chest.

No need to tell them his mother was the last person who'd be worried. She was probably trailing along the lake's edge with her fishing line, with Maddie following in her wake like a small shadow, her own fishing line tangled around the small rod, because to her shells had far more appeal than fish.

But at least his mother would know to listen to messages on the surgery line as well as the home phone when she returned from her excursion.

New voices and laughter preceded the arrival of the ambulance crew, who greeted everyone cheerfully, assured him he'd soon be more comfortable in their care, and then joined the effort of carrying him down to the road.

He was about to lose Lauren Henderson from her place at the head of the stretcher.

As she moved away he reached out with his good hand and caught her fingers. 'I'm sorry for being such a bear,' he said. 'I was just so annoyed with myself for bringing Henry's machine down. It was a stupid and totally irresponsible thing to do.'

She smiled at him. 'It was,' she agreed, but the smile had taken any sting out of her words.

Then she was gone, striding on ahead of the team carrying him down the track.

He wanted to ask about her—who she was, and what she did. She hadn't been sympathy personified, but she'd reset his shoulder—besides which, she was damned attractive.

Knowing someone's name really told you nothing, he was thinking when the paramedic who'd taken her place said, 'The doc reported a dislocated shoulder—looks like she got it back in place. Left one, was it?'

He nodded his reply—mainly because, back in place or not, his shoulder was hurting like the devil, and he really didn't want to be taking any more of the drug.

And why is that? a small voice in his head asked.

He closed his eyes, as if he might shut out the question, but he had a suspicion it might be pride—not wanting these tough men carting his considerable weight down the mountain to think him a weakling.

Stupid pride, at that!

He lifted the little 'whistle' to his lips and took a deep breath.

'Take a few,' said the man at his head. 'Moving you to the ambulance will hurt a bit.'

Cam took a few more puffs. Given the Australian talent for understatement he'd already encountered in his short time here, it was likely going to hurt like hell!

Lauren didn't wait to see her patient loaded into the ambulance. She turned and went back up the path. Telling herself her plan was stupid and futile failed to stop her forward momentum.

As a child, she'd helped Henry—or mainly watched—as he'd built his little ultralight, and it deserved a better end than to be stuck in the burnt-out scrub at the head of the gully. And rescuing the bits would distract her from the reaction she'd felt when the stranger had grabbed her hand and pressed it gently as he'd apologised.

For some reason, that slight touch had left her fingers tingling.

Think about the wreckage!

Even if she couldn't rescue all of it, if she could just recover the frame and the little leather seat Henry had fashioned out of an old saddle…

She thought back to those days when she'd been Henry's little shadow—far closer to him than she'd been to her own father when she was small. Probably because her father's practice hadn't involved animals large and small.

Henry hadn't talked much about his family, although hadn't he once visited a sister or a niece back in England?

Mary?

Marion?

Madge?

It had been Madge—a niece. Maybe she'd inherited the old house and the veterinary practice?

And if he lived with his mother—the tall man with the blue, blue eyes who'd made her spine skitter and her fingers tingle—then that was probably Madge, because the house certainly hadn't been on the market. The lakeside gossip net would have known if it had been.

But living with his mother? Unusual in this day and age... Although she'd lived with her father for years—for ever, almost...

Was he a vet, that tall man with the very blue eyes?

Silly question. Henry had talked occasionally about his great-nephew with a veterinary practice in London—spoken of him with pride. And if she'd ever thought about it, she should have guessed he'd inherit Henry's place and his practice.

But who'd leave London to come to a practice in the bush?

And why should it matter to her, anyway?

Just because he was good-looking?

Because he'd sparked something in her although he'd been abrupt and cranky?

And made her fingers tingle when he'd caught her hand.

And he was going to be living next door.

This last realisation made her feel…not exactly queasy, but unsettled inside.

Puzzling over it kept her feet moving, so she was soon past where she'd met the man, and the wreckage of the ultralight was much more visible—and not as badly shattered as she'd pictured it.

Carefully avoiding any chance of slipping and injuring herself, she gathered up the pieces—one almost complete wing, the bones of the shattered one, and the cockpit, as Henry had grandly called the seat and control panel—and some other bits and pieces not immediately recognisable.

Wishing she'd stopped long enough to get some big bin bags, she untied her light jacket from her waist and tied it around the awkward bundle. She hitched it on to her shoulder and set off, yet again, down the rough track.

By the time she reached her house, drenched in sweat, she was regretting what now seemed like a totally irrational decision.

Just what was she intending to do with the wreckage?

Rebuild the thing?

She dropped the bundle just inside her back gate, unwrapped her jacket and used it to mop the sweat from her face.

'Are you going to put it together again?' asked a quiet, precise voice, and she turned to see a small child with dark tousled hair standing at the fence, dark blue eyes fixed intently on her.

'I'm not sure I'm clever enough,' she answered honestly, seeing the wreckage more clearly now.

'My father could help you,' the little girl told her. 'He knows how.'

Lauren smiled, because the words held such certainty. This was a child who firmly believed her father could do *anything*—although, if the father was who Lauren guessed he was, putting the ultralight back together again was probably the last thing he'd want to do.

Time to change the subject.

'Does your mother know where you are?' she asked.

The small child climbed onto the gate and began to swing back and forth on it. 'I don't have a mother,' she said. 'Daddy said she left to find herself. But I think you *are* yourself, and that's where you are.'

It was slightly convoluted, but Lauren could see where she was coming from, and was amazed yet again at the wisdom of children.

'Do you have a name?' she asked—although she should be asking exactly who was in charge of her, and what she was doing at her back gate.

'I'm Maddie,' she said. 'It's really Madge, after my grandmother, but Daddy says that's a name for an old person not a...' she paused, as if trying out the next word in her head, and finally came up with '...youngser like me.'

'Well, Maddie, perhaps your grandmother is looking for you and you should go home. Do you know the way?'

The girl rolled her eyes. 'It's just next door,' she said, and Lauren thought she heard the echo of an unspoken *Stupid!* lingering at the end of the statement. 'Although it's not as next door as the next door was when we lived in London.'

From London to Paradise Lake. From a bustling, cosmopolitan city to a virtual backwater with a string of houses around a tidal lake. What a huge shift in their lives.

A huge shift in work, too, for the man she'd rescued. From city vet to a country one—and a different country at that.

Had he realised that when he'd come out here?

Did he intend to stay, or merely check out the place and put it on the market?

'I could walk you home,' she offered, concerned about the child, because she'd been quite right. 'Next door' here was about three hundred metres away, and once the sinking sun disappeared it would be gloomy in the sparse bushland between the two houses.

'If you like,' Maddie told her, climbing off the gate. 'We have heaps of baby animals at our place—more than ten, anyway. People come in to help, because some of them are hurt, and some are too little to live in the… Well, we'd say *woods* in England, but here it's called the bush—even if there isn't any bush to live in.'

She waved a hand towards the blackened hills behind them, while Lauren realised that it must be another after-effect of the fires that she'd heard nothing of these new people in Henry's house—not a hint of the gossip which was usually the life-blood of Lakesiders' conversations.

There'd been a locum, of course, and she'd met him one time. And she'd known that volunteers were working all hours to keep the wildlife hospital and sanctuary going. She had done a couple of night shifts there herself, but because she entered and left through the gate in the animal cage, she hadn't met or even considered the new owners.

She took Maddie's hand, and was just leading her to the track she always took between the two places when a tall, dishevelled and totally distracted figure appeared, his left arm held tight to his chest by a sling, his left ankle tightly bandaged.

Campbell Grahame stopped and leaned on the stick he held in his right hand.

'You shouldn't be out walking after that fall,' she said.

But he ignored her, calling out to his daughter and grabbing her as she raced towards him and flung herself at his legs.

'What have I told you about wandering off into the bush?' he demanded, though he didn't sound as cross as she imagined he must be feeling after finding her missing.

'But I only went next door. And this nice lady is going to build the flying machine again after she's walked me home.'

'You must be out of your mind,' he said, and then must have realised he'd already been far too rude to her today. 'Sorry. That was rude. I've been worried about Maddie.'

'I said you'd help her,' Maddie offered hopefully.

The man just shook his head and awkwardly scooped her up with his right arm, his stick now waving uselessly in his hand.

'You should let Maddie walk,' Lauren said, changing the subject before it became even more complicated. 'You shouldn't be bearing your own weight on that ankle, let alone hers.'

He frowned at her, but did let Maddie slide back to the ground.

Okay, the man was in pain, and he must have been worried sick about his daughter's disappearance—but, really, one 'sorry' didn't cover his rudeness.

She looked him directly in the eyes as she responded, daring him to make another prod at her. 'Are you always this aggressive, or has the accident dented your masculine pride? Or is it because you were rescued by a woman?' she asked, aware that it had happened before in the macho world out here in the lakes.

Without waiting for an answer—or an excuse—she turned on the spot and marched back towards her house.

Maddie's, 'Now look what you've done!' came clearly to her through the still, early-evening air. 'And she's a *very* nice lady!'

Beautiful, too, Cam thought as he took Maddie's hand and turned back towards Uncle Henry's house—their house now, he supposed. Not that they *had* to stay here. A few weeks seeing to some necessary repairs, a bit of paint to brighten the place up, and then Cam and his mother could sell it and go back to the UK.

The locum the lawyers had arranged was still running the business and he could stay on—he might even like to buy it. If not, the solicitors could find another buyer.

The thought made him feel even more depressed than the pain in his shoulder. She'd been right, that woman—now soot-stained, probably from rescuing the ultralight—he shouldn't be walking around. But he hadn't wanted his mother to go looking for his daughter—that could have ended up with both of them being lost in the bush...

The bush.

Could he really go back to the UK after seeing the beauty of this lake and experiencing the sense of community around it? Meeting a few of the locals...learning that he owned, apparently, a wildlife hospital and sanctuary, not to mention some of that burnt-out bush behind the house... Henry and some friends of his had planted trees there—a variety of the special trees whose leaves koalas ate—to encourage the local koala population to stay in the area.

For so long he'd dreamt about Australia—this strange land at the bottom of the globe.

Sell out?

He didn't think so.

They were in sight of the house now. The stately old stone building looked so incongruous among the holiday shacks and the new modern houses that straggled along the shores of the lake. He'd learned that it had been built by the owner of a local coal mine, back when the area had first been settled, and the owner had obviously believed strongly in his own importance.

Even with the old servants' quarters at the back now annexed by the wildlife hospital and sanctuary, and his veterinary rooms set up on the ground floor at the front, it was still a lot of house for three people. Spacious and elegant, if somewhat shabby.

'I've forgotten her name…the lady who lives next door…but her house looks even bigger than ours. And there's a sign outside with pictures of cakes. Do you think she's a cake-maker?'

He thought of the tall, slim woman who'd not only popped his shoulder back into its socket but had then also helped carry him down the hill.

'If she is a cake-maker, I don't think she eats many of them,' he said to Maddie.

She grinned with delight. 'Because she's not roly-poly, like Madge says I'll get if I eat too much cake?'

He smiled down at this small human who held his heart in her currently rather grubby hands. 'Exactly,' he said.

And they were both smiling as they entered the house through a French door on one side of it, directly into a rather dim but potentially pleasant sitting room.

* * *

Having shifted the pieces of the ultralight to her back shed, Lauren went upstairs to shower and change. She studied her soot-stained self in the bathroom mirror and shook her head. Pity to have made such a terrible first impression on her new neighbour!

Really? a voice in her head replied. *Why should it bother you what impression you made?*

She didn't answer the voice, not wanting to admit that she'd found him attractive—*very* attractive. And definitely not wanting to admit that seeing him had caused nerves in some parts of her body to jangle, and tighten, and heat— nerves that hadn't felt much for years.

Certainly not warmth.

As for heat…?

Good grief!

What was she thinking?

She sighed. It was because she had no life— that was all it was. Years of medical training, the horrors of internship, and then eight years caring for a wonderful but increasingly difficult father had limited her social life to zilch. No wonder someone—a *male* someone—taking her hand and giving it a gentle squeeze had made her skin tingle.

Had that *ever* happened before out here in the very beautiful but isolated Paradise Lake

community? No. The residents were mostly retired, or newlyweds building their first house
in the place where they'd come for holidays as
children.

Single men were scarcer than hen's teeth, and
as for married men…

Disaster!

But she loved the lake, and she had taken over
her father's practice as well as his care when
his forgetfulness had finally had to be acknowl-
edged as dementia rather than just old age.

Don't brood.

She'd shower, wash her hair, pull on some
jeans and a top and—

And then what?

Take herself to dinner at the new restaurant
that had opened further along the shore?

She shook her head, her wet hair flapping
about her face. Pulled out a dry towel and rubbed
at it roughly, remembering times when she'd
have spent half an hour drying it carefully, persuading it into gentle waves that looked as natural as she could make them.

Looking good for David.

As she dragged a comb through her still-damp
hair, she wondered where that had come from.

It had been years since she'd given David even
a passing thought.

And, more to the point, why was the man she'd rescued today intruding into her brain?

Surely not just because he was an attractive man?

An attractive man who'd made her spine skitter and her skin tingle...

He was a new neighbour, nothing more, and obviously married as he had a child.

Although hadn't the child—Maddie—said something...?

The thought of her encounter with the man at the head of the gully reminded her that she hadn't downloaded her drone's latest pictures. She'd sent the drone home, grabbed her backpack, and then raced off to find whoever it was she'd seen crash.

Glad to have something to do, she went to her office and detached the SIM card from the small machine's belly, pushed it into her computer, and sat down to study what it had picked up.

Nothing much, she decided, when she reached the point where her neighbour had crashed. But as the drone had obeyed her instructions and flown back home before she'd headed out on her rescue mission, it had crossed a new area.

And what was that she could see?

A lump in a burnt-out tree—exactly what she'd been looking for. The lumpy shape of a koala.

She checked the co-ordinates but really didn't need them, for she could see the back fence of the wildlife sanctuary.

She zoomed in.

Could it have come from the sanctuary?

She shook her head.

She'd been there yesterday evening, and knew none of the recovering koalas had been released for over a week. Even those that had been released had gone into suitable forests far removed from the fire grounds.

No, this little fellow—and he or she *was* little—had somehow escaped the worst of the fires and was trying to find a new home.

In a burnt, and therefore leafless tree…

She grabbed a rope and her spiked climbing shoes and hurried towards the sanctuary, wondering who was on duty tonight, hoping it would be someone who could help her.

'Oh, Beth!' she groaned as she let herself in through the security gate in the outer yard. 'Are you on your own here tonight?'

Petite and seven months pregnant, Beth smiled at her. 'Just me, and I'm shutting up soon. The animals that need night feeds have gone home with Helen. There are only two of them, and she says they're pretty good, so she can feed them both at once. The new vet came in to look around early this afternoon, though.'

The new vet with a dislocated shoulder...
although his shoulder wouldn't have been dislocated then...

Henry's great-nephew, with a voice that sent a shiver down her spine.

But was he here to take over the practice, or sell it and move on?

Enough.

She needed to concentrate on the animal in danger. Night was falling fast, and to try a rescue in the dark would be foolhardy, to say the least.

But on the other hand...

She headed for the inner door—the one that led into the veterinary surgery.

His shoulder had been X-rayed and expertly strapped to his chest, and he'd been walking—albeit with a stick...

She knocked on the connecting door, loudly, because it was more likely he was in the house itself and wouldn't hear a gentle tap.

The door opened immediately!

'Yes?' he said, sounding abrupt.

But when she saw the glass beaker in one hand and the pipette in the other, she realised she'd interrupted something he'd been doing.

Following her gaze, he said, 'Sorry. I've just been testing some of the old supplies at the back of the cupboard. I'll be right back.'

She'd have liked to tell him again that he

shouldn't be moving about on his ankle, but as she was about to ask his help in an operation more complicated than beakers and pipettes, she kept her lips firmly closed.

And shut her mind firmly to the man himself who—as a man, for heaven's sake—was causing her more problems than her concern for his welfare.

Internal problems.

Physical problems.

Things she hadn't felt in years.

The shivery spine and tingling fingers had only been the start...

Get with the program!

'There's a small koala, not far from here. My drone picked it up,' she said, as she confronted her grumpy neighbour for the second time—no, third—today. 'The problem is, he's up a burnt tree, and will have realised there's no food, so as soon as it's fully dark he'll climb down and head further into the burnt area and we might not find him again.'

She paused, hoping the look on her new neighbour's face was incomprehension, not disbelief.

She tried again. 'I can climb up and get him. I just need someone to hold the rope and the bag and take him from me so I can climb down.'

He frowned at her, a quick glance taking in

her coiled rope and spiked boots, and the bag she'd grabbed as she'd walked through the sanctuary to his door.

'I know you're not one hundred percent, but I can't ask Beth to help me, and it would take too long to get one of the other volunteers here, so do you think you could? Please?'

The silence seemed to echo through the room, and then he smiled in a way that made her wonder if this was a good idea. Plenty of men smiled at her—but none of those smiles sent warmth bubbling through her veins.

Really, this was getting out of hand!

How could she possibly be attracted to a total stranger?

She was tired—exhausted, in fact—after two treks up the gully today, so it was probably just her imagination anyway.

'I suppose one good turn deserves another,' he said, and smiled again. 'I'll get my walking stick and you can lead the way.'

She threw him her grateful thanks and moved back into the sanctuary, where small wombats poked their noses from old hollow tree trunks and sleepy koalas barely noticed her.

She breathed deeply, smelling the so-familiar scent of eucalyptus leaves, and told herself he probably smiled at everyone that way.

Breathing certainly calmed her nerves, so when he reappeared she was able to say, 'It's just out here—not far,' and lead him out through the side gate of the sanctuary.

She pointed into the second row of the burnt-out plantation. 'Don't look at the tree. Look for the lump in it.'

'Got it,' he said. 'But how do we go about this?'

He lifted the coiled rope off her shoulder, his fingers brushing the bare skin on her upper arm.

'This one's easy,' she said, resolutely ignoring the accidental touch, for all it had shaken her. 'See that branch just below the animal? We throw the rope over that, then I swing on it to make sure the branch will take my weight, rope myself up, and climb. You just have to play out the rope. You're really here just in case I slip, so you can stop me crashing to the ground.'

She took the weighted end of the rope from him and swung it around before flinging it into the tree.

'Okay, the branch looks strong enough. Just let out the rope so the end falls back to the ground, then we'll detach the weight and attach me.'

He played out the rope, but his silence was a little unnerving.

'Sometimes you have to climb up to attach the

rope,' she said—nervous chatter, she knew, but it was better than silence. 'Or attach it in stages as you climb, so if you do fall, you don't fall far.'

She tied the rope around her waist, grabbed the bag, and handed it to him.

'Make sure you hold him by the scruff of his neck when I pass him to you, and the sooner you get him into the bag the better. They're fighters, and their claws are sharp and can really rip into you.'

She headed for the tree.

'And keep one foot on the rope!' she reminded him as she began to clamber up the trunk.

Struck dumb by the rapid sequence of events, Cam could only shake his head. *Keep one foot on the rope*—he understood that part. She didn't want him struggling to put a panicked animal into a bag and forget he was also the brake on her rope.

Stars were beginning to appear in the sky, and his neighbour was already halfway up the tree.

Did she do this often?

He wanted to ask, but also didn't want to distract her—particularly now, as she was persuading the recalcitrant and possible wounded koala to let go of his perch.

Then she started back down, with the animal

making grunting noises—protesting strongly at this treatment.

Cam wound in the rope, secured the coil beneath his feet, and lifted the bag so she could slip the captive into it.

'There!' she said. There was satisfaction in the word, but keeping the animal in the bag—one-handed—was easier said than done.

'You can lift your foot and let me jump down now,' said his neighbour—Lauren—and he realised she was still several feet above the ground.

He lifted his foot and held out his spare hand to steady her as she landed lightly beside him.

'Thanks,' she said, with a smile that made him wonder if this had all been a dream: the beautiful smiling woman, sooty again from the tree, the animal still complaining in the bag, the fading sunset behind the burnt-out forest where they stood and the glimmer of a silvery lake in front of them.

She was not at all the kind of woman who usually sent his body into a perfectly natural male response. Not that this could be compared with anything usual!

The timing couldn't be worse—just settling into a new life, Maddie to think of, a practice to learn and run, a divorce to be settled—yet still she turned him on.

It had to be an enchantment of some kind.

He checked her out again—a quick, sidelong glance—wondering...

'Come on,' she said. 'We have to check him out.'

CHAPTER TWO

'Why do you do this?' he asked, as they walked the short distance back to his house and the wild-life sanctuary.

She turned towards him and even in the near darkness he saw the flash of white teeth as she smiled.

'I suppose because I can,' she answered, adding, 'And I'm good at it.'

He wished he could see her more clearly, read her expression—not that he'd learn much, he guessed.

So he asked. 'How come?'

'I grew up doing it,' she said. 'I don't know how much you know about koalas, but about twenty-five years ago koala numbers were being decimated by the chlamydia pecorum infection. In an attempt to wipe it out large numbers of animals were caught, treated—cured, really—tagged, and rehomed back in the bush. My father and Henry were at the forefront of the effort in this district around the lake.'

'I heard about it and assumed that was possibly why Henry started the wildlife hospital and sanctuary at the back of his house.'

'Your house now, isn't it?'

They were approaching the house, and he looked at it and nodded his head. 'Such as it is,' he said.

She chuckled—such a soft, musical sound he had to smile.

'Mine's worse,' she told him, pausing to drop her climbing shoes and the rope at the edge of the path where it divided to go east and west. They were going west.

'I get builders in,' she said, 'to fix one thing, and they discover a dozen worse problems.'

'You might give me some names,' he said, 'but first—is it too much to ask that you give me a hand with our friend here? I *am* a vet, and I have treated the odd unusual animal back home, but although I've read up on them I've no practical knowledge of koalas.'

He held up the bag, in which a very disgruntled koala was still complaining loudly.

Lauren felt a moment's hesitation, even though she'd fully intended to get the koala sorted before she left.

So, was the hesitation because talking to this man was so easy?

Or because it was so long since she'd had a man to talk to—just talk...?

Stupid!

For a start, he was probably still married—there was the child, Maddie, even if her mother was off 'finding herself...'

And secondly... Well, she'd prefer not to think about the secondly—which was, to put it bluntly, her physical reaction to this man. It had to be the result of prolonged celibacy that had her blood warming when he spoke and her skin tingling if they accidentally brushed against each other.

But she could hardly walk away and leave him with an injured animal and no idea where to begin his treatment of it.

'Of course I'll help,' she heard herself say, hoping she sounded brisk and efficient, and not as dubious as she felt. 'You need time to learn what you can and can't do with wildlife. Just don't lose your heart to any of them—or, worse, let Maddie get too attached. They all go back into the bush eventually.'

He opened the gate into the mesh cage, and in the low light within she saw the grey pallor of his face.

'You've done too much!' she said, cursing herself for her stupidity. 'I shouldn't have asked you to help. We should have let him go—take his chances.'

He shook his head, but she'd already found a stool for him to sit on, and as she guided him towards it, her arm around his back, she took the bag from him.

'Did the hospital check you for concussion or mention you could have it?'

'They asked if I had anyone at home to keep an eye on me, and I assured them I did.'

Not that his mother wouldn't be perfectly capable of caring for him, but she had Maddie to think of as well, and probably wouldn't want to be up and down all night checking on him.

'Well, you just sit for now, but tell me if you start to feel woozy.'

She checked him out as unobtrusively as she could. His colour had certainly returned, and his eyes seemed bright and focussed.

'I won't fall off the stool, if that's what's worrying you,' he said. 'Now, let's get this animal sorted. I'm following the locum around, and beginning to learn what's where in the vet surgery, but I haven't spent more than a few minutes out here.'

Lauren hesitated. There was something about this man—Cam—that made her feel...not uncomfortable, exactly, but disturbed. As if the normally reliable nerves and tissues inside her

were sending messages through her body…
messages she couldn't understand—or didn't
want to.

Nonsense. Get on with it.

'I've done this often enough,' she said, hoping she sounded more casual than she felt. 'And
it will give you a chance to see how to go about
things.'

She hesitated again, now more worried about
his health than the effect he was having on her.

'Do you need something to drink—or some
food? I don't want you fainting. I'd never get you
upright again!'

He smiled at her, sending that strange warmth
through her veins again.

Bloody hell.

She knew what she must look like—tall,
skinny, slightly sooty…well, very sooty, if she
was honest…

And obviously he was just smiling because
she'd been kind. Right?

'I had soup and toast with Maddie earlier,' he
said, 'so no food—though I am glad to get my
weight off my ankle.'

Relieved, Lauren turned her attention to the
animal.

'You probably know all this just from your
general practice, but it'll be quicker and easier
if I do it this time.'

He smiled again.

'I'd never met a koala until I came here a week ago,' he said, waving his hand towards the resident population of eight recovering animals. 'While as for wombats—I'm not entirely sure I'd even dreamt of meeting one.'

'Not covered in your general course at uni?'

He shook his head, the smile still hovering.

Get on with the job in hand, Lauren told herself.

At least that should counter the weird reactions she was having to this man.

Be professional. Big breath!

'Okay, I'm going to have to anaesthetise him to check him out, and it will be easier to do that while he's still in the bag. Would you mind holding it a bit longer while I get what I need?'

She handed him the bag and hit the code to get into the locked storeroom, where medication and equipment were kept. There, she grabbed a syringe and an ampoule of the anaesthetic they used, a mask, and a small cylinder of oxygen, just in case.

'Will you inject into an upper limb?' Cam asked, and she saw he had the animal on his knee.

He had managed to uncover its furry face, and one shoulder, while keeping the claws tucked away in the bag.

'Yes, that's easiest,' she said, and slid the injection into the animal.

'I do know all about cleaning the site before injecting, and all those rules,' she explained as she disposed of the sharps and other rubbish, 'but you have to weigh that up with the stress we're putting on him.'

'Or her,' Cam said, smiling again as he lifted the now comatose koala from the sack.

'What next?' he asked.

Her mind went blank. She had to get out more, if a man's smile was turning her into a turnip-head!

'Now we look at him,' she said, adding quickly, 'Or her.'

She settled the little bear on a clean paper towel on the bench in front of them and checked the body. 'Her,' she said, with confidence this time.

'And start fluids, I would think?' he said. 'Do you give them in a drip or intramuscularly?'

'IM,' Lauren said. 'And regularly—until she's well enough to take water from a dish. If she's been wandering through the fire grounds we can expect burns to her feet, and maybe her face—see here?'

She showed him a small patch of reddened, blistered skin near the snout, then lifted each foot, again red and blistered. But the belly fur, although dark with soot and debris, seemed un-injured.

'If the burns are too extensive, surely you'll have to euthanise?' he said.

Lauren nodded, probing at one of the hind pads that seemed to have a deeper burn.

'These look first-degree, I'd say,' Cam said, and again Lauren nodded, amazed at how quickly she'd relaxed now they were both in a more professional mode.

'Except maybe for this left rear. But at least that means they're easier to treat. We need to soak them first,' she said. 'Ten minutes in a weak saline solution so we can debride any burnt skin before we dress the burns.'

'And just how to you do the soaking part?' her helper asked.

Lauren heard the smile in his voice and looked up. Smiled back. 'Give her a bath,' she said, crossing to the sink and filling a basin with warm water. 'She'd hate it if she was awake, but while she's sedated it's quite easy. She needs all the burnt rubbish out of her fur anyway, before we can check for any other injuries.'

'Maybe you should be the vet here,' Cam said, and Lauren grinned.

'I have been for the last few months,' she said, easing the koala into the basin. 'The fires threw everyone out of kilter, and the locum Henry's lawyers had appointed didn't manage to get here until a couple of weeks ago. But nor did a huge number of our usual holidaymakers, so my practice wasn't as busy either.'

'You're a doctor?'

She lifted the little bear out of the basin and placed her on a towel while she changed the filthy water, returning with a clean dish and pausing to glance at the man who'd asked the question, his head now bent over the bear as he tried to keep all four paws in the water.

'I am—but I didn't tell you that, did I?'

He looked up and grinned, restarting all her physical sensations.

'I think the rescue team and the paramedics all calling you "Doc" was a bit of a giveaway,' he said. 'I owe the whole lot of you thanks for the rescue, but also an apology. I was so furious with myself for doing something so irresponsible as flying the machine, I was positively rude.'

'You were hurting, too,' she reminded him, inordinately pleased by the apology.

He smiled again.

Oh, dear.

'That's no excuse,' he said. 'I knew it was stupid, but Maddie was so excited when I told her I'd flown one before, well…'

A rueful smile this time, but just as effective at jangling her nerves.

If she concentrated on the job at hand she could ignore the smiles, she told herself, and changed the water for the second time.

'There's necrotic tissue turning white on the front paws.' Cam pointed it out to her.

'That's good. We can take her out now, and dry her, and cut off all that dead skin before treating her.'

She dried the small animal carefully, then set her down on a clean towel.

'Can you keep a hand on her while I sort out what I'll need?' she asked.

Cam reached out with his good hand to hold the animal gently, avoiding the damaged areas— learning through touch, Lauren thought, and respected him for it.

Knowing the sanctuary so well, she quickly found what she needed, and gave the little animal her first injection of fluids.

'If I had two hands I could at least do the debriding for you,' he said, but she brushed away his words.

'I've done it often enough that it's almost second nature for me now,' she said as she snipped. 'We use that antibiotic ointment and then a nonadhesive dressing,' she said, as he peered at the different things she'd produced from the cupboard.

'Then you have to bandage them?' he asked, looking up at her.

His head was so close she found it difficult to answer. 'Bandages—of course!' she finally managed, turning away and all but running to the refuge of the supply cupboard. 'We bandage the pads like we'd bandage the palm of a hand, leaving her claws free to hold a grip on her perch.'

The words tumbled out as she began the job, the table between them now.

'And you just leave the nose?' he asked.

Somehow the sensible question settled her nerves, and she was able to glance across at him. 'I think that's your job,' she said. 'What would you do?'

'Leave it and keep applying the cream.'

His voice was beautiful—deep and rich—and the English intonation invested it with something special.

Not rude at all now...

Despite the ache in his shoulder, and a general sense of pain all over his body whenever he moved, Cam found himself enjoying this experience—enjoying being with this woman as well as learning about the treatment of the little bear. Not that they *were* really bears, koalas, but Uncle Henry had sent Maddie a toy one

when she was born, so he'd always considered
them to be bears.

There was something restful about this
woman. Definitely competent, but quietly so,
assured—and confident in her own skin. It was
how he wanted Maddie to grow up—but how
did you achieve that, given things like peer
pressure and the widespread influence of the
dreaded Internet?

'Is something wrong?' Lauren asked, and he
realised he must be frowning.

He shook his head and had to smile. 'I'm letting myself panic about things that might never
happen—worrying about how to bring Maddie
up to be herself and proud of it. Stupid, I know,
when she's only four.'

'A very bright four-year-old, from the little
I've seen of her.'

He sighed. 'Yes, she is that! But so was her
mother.'

A deeper sigh.

'Was?' Lauren asked. 'Her mother's dead?'

He gave a huff of laughter that sounded per-
ilously close to a snort.

'Not dead,' he said, 'but she might as well be
for all the interest she takes in her daughter. She
left us two years ago, certain that some god, or
fate, or some higher power, had a purpose for
her and she had to find it—to… Well, I think

just to save the world, generally speaking. No big challenge! Last I heard she was here in Australia, way up north in the rainforest. Trees are one of the many things she's dedicated to saving.'

He heard the edge of sarcasm in his own voice—weary sarcasm, for there'd been long battles fought on the subject…fought and lost.

'Maddie barely remembers her—which is sad, as she was a good mother when she felt like it, thinking up fun games, telling stories, walking in the park to see the squirrels.'

Was that an echo of sadness in his voice now? He hoped not.

He had realised very early on in their marriage that it probably wouldn't last. The magical, mystical wild child who had so comprehensively spellbound him was, in reality, careless and unreliable, not to mention emotionally fragile, needy, and totally exhausting to be around twenty-four hours a day.

Realising his mind had wandered, he tuned back in to Lauren, who was saying something about the size of their patient—something to do with feeding.

'I'm sorry, I was miles away,' he said, and she smiled.

'That's okay—it's actually a wonder you're

still able to sit there after the fall you had. I was saying I think she's probably feeding mainly on leaves now, but I'll give her some milk because it's easy and should help her settle. We use a soy-based infant formula.'

She waved the feeding bottle she had in her hand and wrapped an old woollen cardigan around the wounded animal, which was just beginning to stir.

'This might make her feel safer—remind her of her mother's pouch,' she explained. 'There,' she added, as she tucked the sleepy animal against her chest and looked down into button-bright eyes. 'Would you like some milk?'

She slid the soft rubber teat into the koala's mouth and Cam reached out and touched the soft fur on her head.

'She really is quite beautiful…damaged paws and all,' he said, in a slightly awed voice.

'She is that!' Lauren said, and they both watched as the little animal investigated the teat with her pink tongue before finally taking some milk. 'Good girl,' Lauren said.

And, although exhaustion was telling Cam he should take himself off to bed, he found he couldn't leave, mesmerised by this woman talking quietly to the injured and undoubtedly traumatised animal. It was a picture he'd probably keep in his mind for ever.

* * *

As the animal's eyes closed, and the teat fell from her mouth, Lauren stood up, mentally wondering where to leave the little koala.

'I'll just settle her in a box under a tree, so she can climb out if she wants to,' she said.

Looking up at Cam as she spoke, she read the grey pallor of exhaustion in his face.

'Oh, for heaven's sake! I'm so stupid—letting you stay here while I sort her out. You should be in bed. I shouldn't have asked for your help.'

She slid the animal into a cardboard box, and pushed it up against a tree trunk that had some fresh green leaves tied to it about two feet above ground level.

'Come on,' she said, moving towards the man on the stool. 'Let me give you a hand back into the house.'

He reached for his stick with his right hand but she waved it away, sliding her arm under his right shoulder to help ease him to his feet.

'Now, put your free arm around my shoulder and lean on me,' she said as he teetered unsteadily.

'I'm really quite all right,' he protested feebly.

'And I'm a Martian,' Lauren retorted. 'Come on—one step at a time.'

The fact that he *was* leaning on her told Lauren just how exhausted he must be. At least he'd eaten and could go straight to bed.

Bed.

Bed was the last thing she wanted to think about, given the way this man she held so closely—for nothing but support, mind—was making her feel…making her body feel.

Forget all that—she'd think about it later. Right now she had to find somewhere for him to sleep—in a house where the bedrooms were all upstairs.

He'd never make it.

'Let's head for your living room,' she suggested. 'In Henry's day there was a good couch in there. It won't be long enough for you, but we can prop your legs up at one end and your head the other and it will save you the stairs.'

'And who is "we"?' he asked.

She turned to look at him—so close she could see the beard shadow on his chin and the tilt of a smile on his lips. 'Me!' she said, possibly with more force than was necessary as she tried to ignore her reaction to those smiling lips. 'Trust me, I'm a doctor!'

Though a fine doctor you are to have let him sit for so long, she finished in her head, as the weight of the man pressed close to her.

It was disconcerting, to say the least.

No, it was far more than disconcerting. But

that was also something she could think about later...

'Nearly there,' she said, far too cheerily, as they crossed the tiled entry and went into the living room, straight towards the couch. 'Now, are you okay to sit?' she asked when they reached it, thinking that if he dropped down onto it too suddenly he might jar his shoulder.

'Very slowly,' he growled, and she knew he understood.

Eventually, with cushions from the armchairs, she had his length settled.

'That's fine,' he said. 'Stop fussing!'

So she did—although she knew the nights got chilly and he would need something to cover him.

She went back into the wildlife hospital area. Locals knitted and donated all manner of things for the animals, and there, in one of the cupboards, she found a couple of bright crocheted blankets.

'They would be pink!' he muttered at her as she spread them over him.

'It suits you,' she said. 'Now—pain relief. Did the hospital give you something?'

'I don't need it,' he said, and she laughed.

'You're doing that man thing of grinning and bearing it,' she teased. 'It's not going to make you look like a wuss if you take a couple of tablets. Where will I find them?'

'Wuss? I'm being a wuss, now?

'*I* think you're being a big baby.'

The small voice made them both turn to see Maddie, in a long nightdress, standing in the doorway, a toy koala tucked under one arm.

'What are you doing out of bed?' her father demanded. 'And where's your grandmother?'

'She's asleep,' Maddie said, coming closer to her father and sidling up until he could put his arm around her small body. 'And I heard voices.'

This probably wasn't the time to tell the child she shouldn't be coming downstairs on her own to investigate voices in the night, so instead Lauren asked, 'Do you know where the tablets your father brought home from the hospital might be?'

Maddie nodded, and handed the toy koala to her father. 'You hold Gummie and I'll show you,' she said, and she headed off out through the door, clearly expecting Lauren to follow.

'I'll get you some water as well,' Lauren said. 'You'll be all right here with Gummie?'

She was smiling as she said it, and although all she received by way of an answer was a baleful glare, she was fairly sure he'd stay where he was. He was in too much pain to do much else, she guessed, as she followed Maddie towards the kitchen.

'I imagine those tablets are up in that cupboard so you can't reach them,' she said, walking into the room to find Maddie dragging a chair towards a high kitchen cupboard.

'Yes, but Daddy needs them,' she said, abandoning the chair and pointing to the cupboard she'd been aiming for.

Lauren retrieved the painkillers, read the label and checked her watch, surprised to find that it was after ten. She'd come for help at about six, so he certainly hadn't had any pain relief in the last four hours.

She washed her hands, then released two tablets from the aluminium strip, filled a glass with water and, herding Maddie in front of her, headed back to the living room.

'Will you stay and look after my daddy in the night?' the child asked, and Lauren looked down and saw the worry in her eyes.

'He really doesn't need looking after now,' she said gently.

Maddie nodded, but Lauren couldn't fail to read the mutiny on her face.

'But I could stay if you'd like me to,' she told the child, who lit up with utter delight.

'I'll stay and help too,' Maddie promised.

And Lauren began to realise it was going to be a very long night.

CHAPTER THREE

'WHAT ON EARTH are you doing here?'

The grouchy question brought Lauren out of her dreams of unburnt forests and back to the real world in a second.

She glanced over at the second armchair, wondering briefly if it was as uncomfortable as hers, but Maddie was still sound asleep. Finally she looked at Cam, who appeared exhausted, dark-jawed, and not very happy.

'There are two painkillers on the table to your right,' she said, 'and some water. You might want them before you try to stand.'

'I haven't time to wait for them to work,' he muttered, squirming as he tried to untangle himself from the crocheted covers.

'Here, let me!' Lauren said, standing carefully as she realised her cramped sleeping position had her own joints complaining.

She crossed the room and disentangled him,

then shifted the cushions that had propped up his legs so he could swivel around and stand.

Handing him his stick, she bent her knees and slid her arm under his right shoulder to help ease him to his feet.

'Just take it slowly,' she warned.

He was pushing against the pain, and would probably have had them both on the floor if a woman hadn't appeared in the doorway.

'He always was stubborn, even as a child,' said the woman—who must be the missing Madge. 'And far too proud to accept a bit of help. Makes him cranky, people helping him. I put it down to losing his father when he was only young—Maddie's age, really. Felt he had to be a man from then on, and hated not being able to do everything his father had.'

Somehow they were upright.

'Thanks, Ma,' Cam growled at the woman, before turning to Lauren. 'Now I'm on my feet, I think I can manage the bathroom on my own.'

'I need to get home anyway,' Lauren said, backing off with her arms up, surrendering. 'I'm Lauren Henderson,' she said, turning to the new arrival. 'I live next door. I stayed because Maddie was worried about her father.'

Aware she must look a sight—still sooty in parts, and wearing slept-in clothes—she headed out of the room, across the entry, and escaped through the front door. It was only when she got to where the paths merged, and bent to retrieve her spiked shoes and rope, that she realised she was starving.

She could vaguely remember having a cup of tea when she'd returned from the gully the second time, and whatever she'd eaten with that had been her final meal of the day.

She should have raided her neighbour's kitchen last night, but by the time she'd settled Maddie in one of the cushionless armchairs, and herself in the other, she'd been too tired even to think about it.

Cam brought the old motorbike slowly out of the scrub and looked up at the mellow yellow of the stone building in front of him.

He lowered his legs to the ground to get his balance.

He also tucked his left hand back into its sling, aware he shouldn't have had it out for even such a short time.

He looked at the building again, seeing it as somehow warm and welcoming.

Had she—Lauren, he reminded himself— had the stone cleaned in some way so that it looked so much better than the drab greyness of Henry's—*his!*—home?

'Just nip inside and ask if we can see the doctor for a minute,' he said to Maddie, who'd dismounted to stand beside him.

She didn't hesitate, disappearing through the front door and turning to speak to someone in the entry. He smiled to himself, imagining the small but determined child doing battle with a receptionist—the guardian of the dragon's lair.

Dragon?

Lauren?

He was spending too much time with Maddie, for whom dragons—mostly friendly—lurked in every corner.

He was just beginning to think he'd have to abandon his means of transport and go in himself when his daughter reappeared, helmet swinging from one hand, the other towing Lauren behind her.

'She had to finish with someone else,' Maddie announced as she delivered her prize to her father.

'Are you *mad*?' the prize demanded, in what seemed like an echo of those other words she'd spoken to him. 'Riding around on Henry's old motorbike with only one hand?'

He shrugged, unwilling to say that yesterday's koala adventure had left his ankle far more painful than his shoulder, especially as she was still frowning at him.

'I did cheat and use the other hand—and the shoulder feels fine. You did a good job!'

She brushed away the compliment, no doubt aware he was buttering her up.

'Isn't there a car?' she asked, then answered herself. 'I guess the locum is using the four-wheel drive, but I'm sure there's another car—'

'Then you might remember the size of it,' he said, and won a half-smile.

'Bit hard to get in and out of?' she guessed. 'Painful, too, I'd imagine. Not that you should be driving with only one hand, so that was a silly suggestion anyway.'

'Anyway, Madge has taken the small car into the village. That's why we're here.'

'You've escaped? Made a dash for it?'

He grinned at her and shook his head. 'My mother,' he said in mock-repressive tones, 'has gone shopping for a leg of lamb. Apparently, women living on their own never cook themselves a leg of lamb.' He paused, and then added, 'Men either, I suppose. But, anyway, she wants to thank you for rescuing me yesterday, and would like you to come to dinner tonight.'

'You assume I live alone?' she asked, eyebrows rising, and he sighed.

Bad enough that he lived with two women—well, one and a half—who argued with him all the time, but now this neighbour—his only close neighbour, his quite beautiful neighbour…

'We were together on our koala rescue mission for several hours last evening and you didn't call or text once. Not a single "I might be late" message, or an incoming phone call from a worried husband, friend, relative, partner…whatever. Then you stayed the night—which, I realise, you did for Maddie, not for me, but still…'

He paused, trying to work out how they'd got so side-tracked.

Back to the subject of his visit. 'So, will you come to dinner? Seven?'

'Madge makes great puddings,' Maddie put in as she pulled on her helmet and clicked the straps together.

'Thank you. I'd be happy to join you,' Lauren said, and he felt a surprising flip of pleasure at the thought. 'But you shouldn't really be moving around too much on that ankle—and get that hand back in the sling as soon as you get home.'

'We rode very slowly, and only on the bush track between our houses.'

'Well, go home and rest anyway,' she said severely, shaking her head at his folly, although he thought he glimpsed the sparkle of a smile in her eyes.

'Yes, Doctor,' he said, raising his hand to his forehead in a smart salute, then turning to settle

Maddie on the bike behind him, checking her helmet was secure.

'We go very slowly,' Maddie piped up, 'because Daddy really doesn't know how to ride a motorbike! He just likes finding things in Uncle Henry's old shed and trying them out.'

He watched Lauren roll her eyes and shake her head, and had to grin. 'It's been a while since I rode a motorbike,' he said.

A call from inside had her turning away.

'Seven,' he called after her, really pleased that she'd left the scene before he kicked the engine into life and wobbled his way down the path.

Lauren was glad she had patients to take her mind off this latest encounter with her neighbour—although, as she should have realised, he was one of the main topics of their conversation.

'It's nice to have some young people up this end of the lake again, isn't it?' said Mrs Brimble-combe, while Lauren took her blood pressure.

'Aren't you counting me as young?' she teased, smiling at the woman she'd known since she was a child.

'Of course you're young,' her patient said. 'But there's the new vet, and Kelly, who's started that café just along the shore a bit, and Beth and her new baby coming…'

Lauren wrote out the prescription Mrs B had

come for while the lady listed all the young people and families who had moved to this end of the lake in the last six months, and although Lauren only half listened, it still seemed a lot.

How had she not noticed it, this influx of youth?

Because you're no longer what most people would consider a youth, she reminded herself.

But as she saw Mrs B out through the door and ushered in another elderly local—Mr Clarke—her mind was back on the new vet.

Now, he *was* young.

She wondered how long a veterinary course might be in the UK—here it was five years, longer if one wanted to specialise, but over there—

'I was asking if you had all the pieces,' Mr Clarke said, quite sharply, alerting Lauren to the fact that she'd missed quite a bit of his conversation.

'Of the ultralight?' she guessed.

'Of course the ultralight,' Mr Clarke said. 'I was saying I might be able to help you put it back together. A few of us thought we could help. As a tribute to Henry, you know.'

Am I that old, she wondered, *that aged pensioners of the area are offering me their help?*

'I'll have to have a good look when I have some time,' she said, aware of the lameness of her answer.

But if she accepted their help she'd be committing to endless mornings or afternoons listening to discussions on their bowel problems, or comparisons of their drug routines. She'd had experience of that on the rare occasions when she'd dropped into the sailing club for a drink.

She'd been thinking the rebuilding of the ultralight would be a break away from work...

She fixed her mind on her patient, listening to his list of symptoms, sloughing off the purely irrelevant items on the list, like the funny noises in his left ear, and deciding, after she'd done the regular checks, that there wasn't anything much wrong with him.

'Although you do have quite a build-up of wax in both ears,' Lauren told him. 'I can easily syringe them out.'

'My mother told me that you should never put anything smaller than your elbow in your ear,' her patient said, then he smiled. 'I suppose that's silly, because you can't get your elbow into your ear, can you.'

He proceeded to try the process with both elbows and both ears, while Lauren quietly prepared what she'd need.

'It's not that I mind that they're all so healthy,' she said, over a delicious dinner of roast lamb.

'It's just that occasionally I'd like—I don't know—perhaps a challenge.'

'Be careful what you wish for,' Madge said to her. 'That one—' she nodded towards her son '—can get into trouble just sitting at his desk. I mean, how many vets do you know who've been bitten by a tiger?'

'It was a very small tiger,' Cam said quickly, but Lauren was shaking her head in disbelief.

'A tiger?' she echoed.

'It was at the zoo,' Cam said, defensive now. But he could see he wasn't going to get away with that. The gleam of mischief in Lauren's dark eyes told him that much, while that same gleam raised far too many disturbing sensations within his body.

Attracted to the girl next door—what a cliché!

'And it was just a cub,' he said, hoping his voice sounded less distracted than his mind was.

Lauren was hanging on Madge's every word, her lips quirked into a teasing smile, loving these tales of him as a foolish young student.

'A cub bite that put you in hospital for a week,' Madge reminded him, relishing his embarrassment.

'It had bad teeth.'

He was even more defensive now, but the

smile on Lauren's face told him she was enjoying this as much as Madge.

Not that he minded Lauren smiling and laughing at him.

In fact, his earlier impression that she was
beautiful was enhanced by that smile.

'Pardon?' Lauren had spoken. He shouldn't
have been thinking about her smile.

He had far too much on his plate, what with
learning about the practice while the locum was
still here, settling Maddie into school, and just
generally getting himself organised. He had to
do something about Maddie's mother, too! Get
that part of his life organised. She wasn't coming back, so it was time he insisted she sign the
divorce papers.

How could he concentrate on all these things
if a simple smile from a woman he barely knew
threw him into a spin?

'I wondered if it was septicaemia that had you
in hospital?' Lauren was asking, the smile still
lingering in her eyes despite the fact that septicaemia was a serious issue.

He shrugged, and took a gulp of the red wine
he'd found in the cellar. 'They didn't say so, but
it had to be something similar.'

'Poor you,' she said, with a slighter smile this
time, taking a decorous sip from her wine.

'And then there was the elephant seal,' Madge reminded him.

Cam looked apologetically at Lauren. 'Once she's started thinking of all the most embarrassing moments of my life it's hard to stop her.'

'Oh, but I'd love to hear about the elephant seal,' Lauren said.

He knew she was teasing…quite liked it, in fact. But it was time to bring this to an end.

Right now his life was complicated enough, without introducing a smiling, teasing and, yes, tempting woman into it.

If Kate would only sign those divorce papers…

He pushed the thought away and joined the conversation.

'Next thing we know we'll be back in my childhood, with Madge bringing up my being chased by the Loch Ness monster.'

'*Were* you chased by it?' Lauren asked, with so much merriment dancing in her eyes that he wanted to kiss her.

'He only *thought* it was the monster,' Madge put in—which, Cam knew, would only make Lauren more determined to pursue it.

'Oh, look at the time,' he said. 'Please excuse me for a few minutes. I've got to read Maddie's bedtime story.'

'I want Lauren to read it.'

The determined voice from the top of the stairs suggested she'd been there for some time.

'No—' he began, but Lauren was already pushing back her chair.

'I'd love to—if you'll both excuse me? That lamb was delicious, Madge. I'll be back soon.'

'She's in the small bedroom to the right of the stairs,' Cam said, then took a very deep breath and looked at his mother.

'Really, Ma you didn't have to trot out all those stories.'

'Nonsense, she loved them,' Madge replied, her face alive with delight. 'She's really nice, isn't she? And Poppy, the young woman who was in the sanctuary today, says she's single.'

'Ma!' Cam said, turning quickly to make sure Lauren hadn't escaped from Maddie after only one story.

'Well, it's time you started thinking about marrying again. Maddie needs a mother, and I can't stay with you for ever. I've got my own life to lead.'

'Maddie's already got a mother,' he reminded her. 'She could still return!'

'Do you want her to?'

'I don't know,' he muttered, but the new image in his mind of a laughing woman with warm brown eyes told him that answer wasn't entirely true.

Glory be, he thought. *Who knew Uncle Henry's bequest would lead to such a dilemma?*

The story was about a family going on a bear hunt, and as Lauren read she wondered what it would be like to have a family—to be part of one. A family with children like Maddie, always interested and keen to know things.

Like so many children who'd grown up without a mother and without siblings, she'd often dreamed of having a family of her own. And then, what seemed like a very long time ago, she'd had…not dreams so much as expectations that all those things would happen.

Engaged to David, expecting life to spread out before her in the seemingly normal way… for her, nearly through her medical degree, 'normal' had seemed like a wedding, children, family holidays here at the lake.

Caring for a beloved parent with Alzheimer's hadn't been in the plan, and it certainly hadn't fitted in to David's plans. But how could she have walked away from the man who'd brought her up—been mother and father to her? And how deep could David's love have been that he'd refused to countenance any compromise?

That had hurt the most.

Would Cam…?

She batted away thoughts of Cam—it was a

totally senseless comparison. She might be attracted to him, but surely that was just physical. And even if it wasn't, he was far too young for her—there had to be a ten-year gap between them, and the memory of David—the pain of losing him—still lingered deep in her subconscious...had left a lack of trust...

'You missed a page,' Maddie told her, bringing her back to the present with a jolt.

She turned back, read the page, and eventually finished the story, by which time Maddie was sound asleep. But sitting there, watching the sleeping child, made her wonder if she really wanted to go back downstairs.

She felt at peace—something she was unlikely to feel in the vicinity of Campbell Grahame who, with his eruption into her life, had stirred all kinds of strange sensations within her. Sensations she hadn't felt or even thought about for years, and definitely shouldn't be thinking about now. He was a married man with a child, and presumably his wife could return—having found herself—at any time.

A memory of Maddie's voice telling her that Madge made lovely puddings reminded Lauren that said pudding had probably been made and, as a guest, she would be required to at least sample it.

She headed back downstairs, aware of how

familiar the house was to her, and yet now, with its new inhabitants, unfamiliar as well.

'It's a nursery pudding, really,' Madge announced as Lauren came back into the room. 'Just bread and butter pudding. But the family love it, and I know Cam will always sneak a bit when he can't sleep and is wandering the house in the middle of the night, wondering how he came to be sharing his life with so many strange creatures.'

So he had nights like that, too? Only when it was her she was usually wondering about getting the guttering fixed, and whether she could afford to have that done, *and* the chimney swept before winter.

'I don't suppose you can give us the name of a good chimney sweep?'

The question, seeming to come directly from her thoughts, startled her, and she stared at the man, trying to see some sign that he could actually read her mind.

Freaky!

'I thought Maddie would like to have a real fire to sit in front of, make toast and snuggle up, even if it doesn't really get cold enough to justify it.'

'Oh, it gets cold enough,' Lauren assured him, seizing on a bit of the conversation that was easy to answer.

'Then we'll need the chimney checked,' he said. 'Henry might not have used it for years.'

'I do know someone. I need to get him to check mine anyway, so I'll give him a call and let you or Madge know when he can come.'

Good, rational conversation.

Far better than considering the effect this man was having on her, or debating with herself over David's desertion...

'This pudding is delicious, Madge. And you're right—not only do I never bother to cook roast lamb for myself, but it's years since I made a dessert of any kind.'

'Then you must come every Tuesday,' Madge announced. 'That's always our roast night.'

Did she want to get so involved with these people?

See more of Cam in a domestic setting like this?

Some instinct—self-preservation—suggested not.

She was well over David now, and she had a new and different—not to mention extremely busy—life. But that didn't mean she'd forgotten the pain of his rejection—the pain of loving and losing, the talk in the gossip-starved Lakes area.

'She's not wearing the ring any more...'

'I heard he's taken up with someone else...'

The gossip had reverberated through the community, exacerbating the pain and her feelings of loneliness. To go through that again…

'We'll see,' she said. 'Things are quiet at the moment, but come the school holidays, when all the city people arrive, I'm usually too busy for anything regular.'

To prevent further pressure from Madge, she turned to Cam, who'd been concentrating far too hard on his pudding.

'How's our little koala today?' she asked. 'Have you seen her?'

He looked up and smiled at her, as if well aware of why she'd changed the conversation.

'She's well, and eating leaves,' he said. 'The volunteers who were there today tell me we have to change the dressings on her paws every two days, so I'll do that tomorrow and check the wounds. And we had a baby wombat brought in today. I've read up, over the years, on the animals Henry talked of in his letters, but I had no idea they could be so small…and almost totally hairless. Maddie and I both fell in love with it.'

'They're born about the size of a jelly bean, and then they crawl up into the mother's pouch—which, in wombats, is backward-facing, so it doesn't fill up with stones and dirt as she shuffles along. They attach to a teat there, and it kind of swells in their mouth to keep it attached until it's big enough to occasionally poke its head out.'

'A backwards pouch?' Cam sounded totally incredulous. 'In all the reading I've done I've never picked up on it being a backward-facing pouch.'

He shook his head, smiling at the thought, and she rushed into practical speech to avoid thinking about his smile.

'It makes sense—but what had happened to the mother of your new arrival?' Lauren asked, knowing that very small hairless wombats should still be tucked into their mother's pouch.

'Hit by a car,' Cam told her. 'But thankfully the driver had enough sense to check the pouch.'

Lauren smiled. 'Enough sense and enough knowledge,' she said. 'For many years Henry had a ten-minute slot at the end of the local news once a week, and besides showing some of the animals the sanctuary cares for, he educated people on the animals themselves.'

Cam laughed. 'Judging from the number of animals we have in the sanctuary at the moment, he did a very good job of it. And who'd have thought there was a special formula product developed just for baby wombats?'

'You don't know the half of it. Wait till you have to feed a snake.'

He looked at her in horror. 'No—no way! I draw the line at snakes. In fact, I didn't know people would bring them in.'

Lauren smiled at him. 'They don't. I was teasing. Although there is a family on the other side of the lake that handles snakes. If you ever have one in the house, there should be a phone number for the snake-catcher on that board by the phone.'

Cam was shaking his head. 'Snakes in the house? I'm going back to England! That damn ultralight nearly killed me, Henry's motorbike would never pass a safety test, and now you're telling me snakes might come into the house?'

'Not often,' Lauren said, trying not to smile as she teased him. 'And not if you keep the fly screens on your doors closed—which you really have to do, mainly because of the mosquitos.'

Cam groaned and held his head in his hands.

'Take me home, Ma!' he pleaded.

And now Lauren did laugh. Madge called him a wimp and joined in.

'I must be going,' Lauren said when they'd all settled down again, although Cam was still muttering about the dangers of life in Australia. This was a different Cam—light-hearted and fun to be with. And dangerous, given her reaction to this new version of him.

'You didn't even mention the spiders that can kill a person with one bite,' he grumbled, still complaining. 'I hope I'm not expected to look after them as well!'

'Oh, no,' Lauren told him cheerfully. 'The snake man does them too. He's an accredited breeder and handler, and he milks them for the development of anti-toxins.'

Cam shuddered, but as Lauren had got to her feet, and was helping Madge clear the table, thanking her for a wonderful meal, it was obvious she was about to leave.

'I'll walk you home,' he said.

She turned to him. 'It's a couple of hundred metres on a path I've known all my life,' she said. 'Besides which, you should still be taking it easy on that ankle.'

'Oh, let him walk you home,' Madge said. 'His ankle's fine and it will keep him out from under my feet in the kitchen. He's got no idea how to stack a dishwasher.'

Madge wasn't lying. Normally he'd go into his office and write up the day's work—such as it had been—while she tidied. The locals were still understandably nervous about bringing their pets to a new vet, even if he was related to Henry, so continued to see the locum.

But Ma pushing him to walk Lauren home?

By a silvery lake that shimmered in the moonlight?

What could possibly go wrong? a sarcastic voice whispered in his head.

'You really don't have to come with me,' Lauren said quietly as they left the house together.

'You want me to sneak back into the house and hide from my mother?' he grumbled.

She smiled, and all the small snapshots of Lauren he'd taken in his head over the last few days were highlighted by that smile. With her well-proportioned features and that fall of golden hair—he'd been fooled that first day by her dark eyes and brows—she really was quite beautiful.

And he was—

What?

Smitten?

Good grief!

That was far too strong a word.

Maybe it was just fascination—she was so unlike any woman he'd ever known.

And beautiful.

Maybe it was just lust. Although he didn't think lust would have him waiting, almost breathless, for her smile. Or wanting to hear her voice, speaking quietly, just to him, no matter the topic. And surely it had to be more than lust when the teasing glint in her eyes could leave him mute.

He knew for sure that this, whatever this was, had never happened to him before. Not with girlfriends, or Maddie's mother—anyone, in fact. Yet here he was, walking one step behind her, wanting to reach out and clasp her hips. Or walk alongside her so he could sling an arm casually around her waist and then, as their pace slowed, turn her to him and kiss her in the night-scented bush.

His heart was hammering in his chest, while his mind was lost in lustful imaginings.

Control—he needed control.

He stepped into her before he realised she'd stopped, and she turned around, a little frown on her face.

'I was just saying the path's wide enough for us to walk together, rather than you trudging behind,' she said. 'Is your ankle bothering you? Should you turn back?'

Given the strength of his imaginings, it was all he could manage just to shake his head and move up beside her. To find his voice.

'Why aren't you married?'

It was unfortunate, finding his voice right then! Of all the things to have come blurting out. She'd think him mad!

But the question was out, hanging in the air between them like words in a balloon in a comic.

Idiot!

She studied him for a moment, then smiled. 'Did you actually mean to ask that?' she said.

Hoping he didn't look as embarrassed as he felt, he shook his head, then rushed into more speech. 'No, and I'm sorry. That was very rude and none of my business. I don't know what I was thinking. Can we just forget I asked?'

She smiled again, and tucked her hand into his arm to get him started on their journey once again.

'That's okay,' she said. 'I get asked often enough that it doesn't offend me. I just haven't had time.'

He waited. There'd be more, he was sure. But she—they—walked on as if everything had been explained.

'You haven't had time?' he said finally.

'That's right,' she said, totally at ease—or seemingly so—while he was floundering like a fish cast ashore by a rogue wave.

'So, you've nothing against it as such—marriage?'

He'd obviously lost his mind, gabbling on like this, especially as they'd come out of the scrubby bush now, and could see the shimmering lake spread out in front of them.

How had marriage got into the conversation?

It was none of his business why this beautiful woman was or wasn't married.

But the question hadn't had her storming off, removing herself from close contact with a madman. She'd slowed down, and was looking out at the lake in all its glory as she answered.

'Not really,' she said. 'Things just got in the way at the time when marriage was happening to everyone around me. And once all your friends are married, you realise that the pool of available men has greatly decreased—especially when you live in a community as widespread but small as the Lakes.'

Her voice was so even, so placid, she might have been discussing a business venture or even a shopping list, yet underneath the words he heard an echo of...sadness?

So when she changed the subject, saying, 'It's really beautiful, the lake, in all its moods, but I love it in the moonlight—it's so serene...' how could he not slip his arm around her waist and draw her closer to him.

Close enough to kiss.

Had she felt it too? That sudden surge of physical attraction that had him turning her towards him, easing her closer to his body, feeling her softness matching his harder planes?

He kissed her neck, nuzzled it for a moment, and felt her shiver from the touch. So when they did kiss, the power was there—the attraction, or the lust, or whatever it was between them—and it stole his breath, leaving him speechless.

When she eased away he let her go, resuming his place by her side, putting his arm around her waist—walking her home in the moonlight.

They wandered more slowly now, his arm still around her waist, and he felt like a schoolboy walking his first girlfriend home.

Lauren was relieved when the roof of her house loomed above the bushes.

Nearly home!

She could feel the tension in the man who walked so close beside her and knew her own matched it. She really needed to get inside—to put some space between them and work out just what was going on.

First his question about marriage.

And then *that kiss*!

It had not only left her breathless, but also lost, somehow.

What did it mean?

And, more puzzling, why on earth had she responded? She had kissed him back—felt his need and her own hunger…

'As if!'

'As if…?' he echoed, and she realised that her final thought had actually come out of her mouth.

'I really don't know,' she said, reaching her front gate and turning towards him. 'Just random thoughts chasing through my head and then—'

'As if?'

He repeated it with a smile and she looked at

him, standing there in the moonlight, tall and solid—a good-looking man who'd turned up in her life a bit like a genie out of a bottle and ruffled the waters of her usually calm existence.

And she'd kissed him!

Well, he'd kissed her, but she'd definitely kissed him back, reawakening desires she'd thought forgotten, if not long dead. Making her think impossible things, dream impossible dreams...

She barely knew him, and he had a ton of baggage in his life, yet already he'd not only got under her skin, he'd somehow sneaked deeper, into parts of her that had been locked away for a very long time.

'Thank you for walking me home,' she said, and slipped away before she did something foolish—like give him another quick kiss goodnight!

Inside the house, she turned on the lights, determined not to peek through the window and see if he was still there.

Instead, she leant her back against the door, her legs still trembling slightly, and then slid down to sit on the floor, hugging her knees with her arms and wondering about age and levels of maturity...

CHAPTER FOUR

'THIS IS MADNESS,' Lauren muttered to her receptionist as she showed out the fifth patient of the morning and realised the waiting room was still full.

'They mainly want to gossip about the new vet,' Janet whispered. 'Seems they all know you had dinner there last night!'

Shaking her head at the speed of the Lakes' bush telegraph, Lauren sighed. 'Yes, but their excuse is that they need new prescriptions, which I then have to write out—*after* actually checking to see they're okay.'

She bit back another sigh. It was her own conscience making her a little tetchy. She'd slept badly, thoughts of the man next door crowding in her head, and now she found herself overbooked with patients who really only wanted to gossip. Not that she could blame them; any newcomer was newsworthy around the Lakes.

'I think I'm next—when you finish chatting,' a loud male voice declared.

'And I'll be right with you, Mr Richards,' Lauren answered. 'Just go through to the nurse's room and she'll take your blood pressure.'

'Which will be sky-high with all this waiting,' the man grumbled, but he did move in the direction of the small treatment room presided over by Judy, who had been Lauren's father's nurse before Lauren had even started.

At least Judy wouldn't put up with his complaints!

'His blood pressure *is* high,' Judy said, just minutes later, when she showed Mr Richards into Lauren's room.

Lauren sighed and looked at the figures Judy had entered into the computer.

'Mr Richards,' she said, smiling in what she hoped was a persuasive manner, 'won't you even consider Meals on Wheels? If only for a few weeks? You'd be amazed how much better you'll feel.'

His florid face grew even redder, until he seemed to glow from some inner fire. 'I eat perfectly well,' he told her, in a voice that brooked no argument.

But she had to try!

'You don't really,' Lauren argued, patiently and politely. 'You eat a pie and chips or fish and chips at every meal. The only reason you're not even more overweight is that you have to walk to the fish market for your fish and chips, or to the bakery for your pies.'

'I get the pies frozen at the supermarket now. Chunky steak, frozen in packs of four, and you can get chips there too—in the freezer section.'

Lauren heard the silent *so there* at the end of his sentence, and only just managed to stop another sigh escaping.

'You can also get fruit and vegetables at the supermarket while you're there—you can even get them in the frozen section, so all you have to do is cook the veggies and unfreeze the fruit. There's mango, and berries of all kinds, some melon… If you just add a *little* variety to your diet it would be a help.'

Mr Richards scowled at her. 'I get by,' he said.

'With a blood pressure that's off the charts, and forty kilos overweight, you won't be getting by for much longer,' she reminded him—they'd had this conversation almost weekly for *so* long.

'Mightn't want to!' her patient retorted.

Lauren was struck dumb.

Was he saying he deliberately abused his body because he would rather be dead? Did he even take the medication she was already prescribing for him?

She thought back to when she'd first seen him

as a patient, more than ten years ago. He'd only recently retired then, turning his farm over to his son and coming to the lake so his son could run it as he thought best.

Mr Richards had been fit and healthy—with slightly high blood pressure and still recovering from his wife's death some years before. But he'd had his dog, brought with him from the farm...

'Is it because you miss Bonnie?' she asked quietly, and caught the look of pain in his eyes. 'Why not get another dog?' she asked. 'Then you'd have plenty of exercise and training a pup would keep you busy. Your Bonnie was one of the best-mannered dogs I've ever met. The residents at the nursing home loved having her visit.'

Mr Richards eyed her suspiciously, but she sensed interest in her suggestion.

'And where would I get a dog? Bonnie came with me from the farm,' he said, still querulous, but softening.

'I'll ask around,' she said gently, 'and let you know. Now, buy some fruit and vegetables at the supermarket on your way home. You'll have to get used to eating them, because I know Bonnie always loved a slice of apple—and you once told me she also ate vegetables.'

He looked dubiously at her, taking the prescription she'd written and studying it.

'I mean it,' she said. 'I'll find you a dog if you

start to eat more healthily and get yourself a bit fitter. Get up to the bowls club on Friday afternoons and try the barefoot bowls they play there, with people of all ages. It's fun, and you might decide to take up the game.'

'Hmph,' was all he said.

But she felt she'd possibly jolted him enough to start taking care of himself. And when he actually put out his hand to shake hers before he left—just as he always had years before—she felt she might have won a small victory.

Now all she had to do was find a dog!

Ask a vet, was the immediate answer to that problem, but even thinking about Cam brought heat to her face.

She'd put up a notice at the Community Hall instead.

The patients kept coming, so the usual midday closing of the morning surgery stretched closer to one, and she was rostered on at the wildlife sanctuary from one-thirty.

Ask a vet, her head reminded her, but the more sensible part of her brain told her she could quite easily get into the sanctuary through the side gate and needn't see Cam at all.

Memories of the kiss came flooding back, along with the heat she'd felt earlier.

She shook her head, as if that might clear it—

might stop her feeling like a teenager reliving her first kiss!

How on earth had she come to respond as she had?

Attraction, she admitted to herself. It happened between men and women. It just hadn't happened to her for a long time—lying dormant at first, to give her time to heal from the pain of David's loss, and then deadened by her need to concentrate on her father's well-being more than her own.

Why on earth was it affecting her now?

Be sensible. Look at it without emotion.

That was her sensible self talking.

So, yes, he was intelligent, and good company...when he wasn't in pain and grumpy about it. And attractive. *Very* attractive.

Taller than she was—a huge plus for a tall woman—*and* about ten years younger than her. They hadn't discussed age, but she had learned he'd married while still at university.

And, apart from that fairly significant—to her—issue, did she really want another man in her life?

Want to go through the highs and lows of... what?

Falling in love?

That was what teenagers did!

Surely she was too old for such a thing.

Although, would it be such a bad thing?

Falling in love?

She sighed; it was a default setting with her now, the sighing.

If she was honest, it was cowardice holding her back—she was afraid. Not of love itself, but of the power it gave someone else over her, and anyway the whole idea was ridiculous.

'As if!' she muttered to herself.

She made herself a sandwich and a cup of tea, concentrating on thinking about the patients she'd seen to avoid any further thoughts of the vet.

Although... Patients!

All of them had heard about her rescue of Cam and, while most of them wanted to find out all they could about the new arrivals in their small community, a few of them had been focussed on their own problems.

She had given those patients her full attention, aware that it was often in what was left unsaid that she could pick up on what was truly bothering them.

Beth was getting painful Braxton-Hicks contractions, and worrying that they might mean she'd have a premature baby.

Lauren had assured her that they could start any time from the third month, and told her that, yes, they could be painful. But she wasn't certain she'd allayed Beth's fears. She'd examined her carefully, assured her that the pregnancy was proceeding exactly as it should, and reminded her that she—Lauren—was only ever a phone call away should Beth have any concerns.

And Muriel Carter, a spry eighty-year-old, was getting more frequent occurrences of atrial fibrillation. They didn't worry her unduly, although the disturbance made her feel tired, but her daughter, who was a doctor, had wondered if she should have a surgical ablation—a procedure in which tissue in the atria was scarred by extreme heat or cold to stop the electrical impulses that caused the fibrillation.

Lauren had gently pointed out that the operation, involving a wire entering the heart through a blood vessel in the groin, didn't guarantee success. In fact, only about sixty-five per cent were successful. But she'd written a referral for Muriel to take to a heart specialist in Riverview, the nearest big city, and suggested she discuss it with him.

Finishing her sandwich, Lauren rinsed her cup and plate and left them to dry on the sink.

She considered changing out of her 'professional' outfit of trousers and a neat shirt, then told herself not to be stupid and headed for the sanctuary, which was—blessedly—Cam-free.

Helen, who ran the place, greeted her with the news that their latest 'baby' was doing well, and that Cam had been in to replace the dressings on the little koala's paws.

'He seems a really nice man,' Helen said, before taking Lauren around all the animals currently in their care, pausing at one of the young swamp wallabies. 'I think this one might be ready to be released,' she said, 'but you remember how young he was when he came in? He'd never been out of his mother's pouch. And although we've all been taking him outside onto grass in different places, he's really just a big sook, and he always comes back to whoever's taken him out.'

'And you're wondering if he'll manage on his own?' Lauren asked.

'Will you know if he doesn't?' a deep voice asked, and they both turned to see Cam standing behind them.

'Not really,' Helen admitted, and the dejection in her voice told Lauren that she really didn't want to let the little fellow go.

'What about Amanda, who often does the night feeds for us? Lauren suggested. 'She lives up at the swampy end of the lake, where these fellows belong. She might take him to her place for a few days, then leave her back gate open for a while so he can come and go until he gets used to it.'

'Brilliant!' Helen smiled with delight. 'I don't know why I didn't think of it. I'll phone and see if she's home, and if she is I'll take him up right now.'

Helen bustled into the office, leaving Cam and Lauren alone and, as far as Lauren was concerned, acutely embarrassed.

Because they'd shared a kiss?

Or because she'd responded to his kiss?

It was definitely her response making her feel embarrassed right now—it had been as if his lips on hers had released some spark of passion she hadn't known was there! And now the memory of the damn kiss was stuck in the forefront of her mind, the heat it had generated gathering again in her body.

For heaven's sake, she was a mature woman— she needed to get over it!

'Do you fret this much about all the animals you care for?' Cam asked.

Delighted to have a normal conversation, Lauren said, 'The wallabies more than the others. Koalas aren't particularly sociable, and we just release them into a patch of forest that has the type of eucalyptus leaves they eat, and a small colony of koalas within it, and they seem to find their own way back into normal life. And kangaroos don't seem to notice an extra one joining their mob. But these little fellows…'

She slid her hand under the small animal's chin and tilted up his head.

'Look at that face! These are also called Pretty Face Wallabies, and they tend to worm their way into your heart.' She paused, then admitted, 'Well, Helen's heart! I'm more a wombat-lover myself. There's something so self-sufficient about them.'

He cocked an eyebrow, as if to say *just like you*, but she ignored it and began to check the whiteboard, which showed what would need to be done on her shift. It appeared to be mainly cleaning and checking stock.

'Did you want something?' she said, turning back to Cam, who was still standing just inside the door.

'Well, yes,' he said. 'But just information, really.'

He paused, and Lauren wondered what kind of information *she* could give him.

'I was wondering,' he said, eventually, 'where one could take someone out for dinner in this area. Are there any good restaurants anywhere close?'

Maybe he means Madge, Lauren told herself,

even as a niggle of something she didn't want to think about unsettled her equilibrium.

'Well, it depends,' she began. 'You know the village…?'

'The cluster of shops and houses at the near end of the pier?' he asked.

She nodded and smiled, and said, 'We call it the jetty. I don't think it's grand enough to be a pier.'

He returned her smile, and what little equilibrium she'd managed to find all but fled.

Deep breath!

'Yes, that's the village, and towards the end of it—'

'I thought *we* must be the end of it—there are no houses that I've seen beyond mine.'

'We're the western end,' she said, desperate to keep the conversation on something safe, like eating places, so she didn't have to think about last night. 'But on the other side of the jetty, right on the lake, there's a café-type restaurant. It hasn't been open long, but it seems to be gaining a faithful following and a reputation for good food.'

'Eastern end of the village…right,' he said, as if he was mentally writing it down.

'And if you want something a bit more posh then there's the dining room at the golf club. Do you know where that is?'

'It's behind the school. I saw it when I took Maddie up there the other day. Apparently, she's old enough to start there in the kindergarten class, but she doesn't think she should be relegated to that when back home she's going to a real school.'

Lauren had to smile. She could just see Maddie making her point about such a demotion to what she might consider 'little kids' school'.

'Is she still going to start there?' she asked, and Cam nodded.

'Of course,' he said, with great dignity. 'I do still have *some* control over a four-and-a-half-year-old.' Lauren was still smiling when he added, 'Though for how much longer, I don't know. I swear she's four going on forty!'

'She's a great kid,' she said. 'And now I really must do some work. I have patients again from four till six, and if I don't finish my chores here Helen will get cross.'

'Rubbish!' Helen said, emerging from the office. 'You and the other older volunteers are the only ones I trust to do their jobs right. I swear some of the young ones come just so their boyfriends or girlfriends can meet up with them here—probably without their parents knowing.'

Smarting slightly over the 'older volunteer' status she'd been given—heaven knew, some of the other volunteers were in their sixties and seventies—Lauren nevertheless began her cleaning, picking up the straw that had been strewn on the ground in the early morning and bundling it into bags.

Cam's voice startled her. She'd thought he'd left but, no, he was right there beside her, bundling straw into a bag.

'So, if you work till six, would seven be all right? I've discovered the four-wheel drive car the locum has been driving is actually Uncle Henry's—so mine, in fact. I'll call for you at seven?'

Lauren straightened up, clutching none-too-clean straw in one hand, a bin bag in the other.

'Call for me? Whatever for?' she said, glad Helen had already left to deliver the wallaby to his new home.

'To take you out to dinner,' he said, as if it was the most obvious thing in the world.

'Out to dinner? Me?'

He shrugged awkwardly, given the sling still holding his shoulder in place. 'On a date?' he offered, managing in spite of his height and solid build to look sheepish.

'On a date?' Lauren echoed, but weakly, because even as she said it she knew there was nothing she'd like more than to go out to dinner with Cam.

As a friend, of course.

But a *date*…

The very idea caused a sizzle up her back-bone—which, surely, should be a warning not to go? Not to get too involved.

He's married, she reminded herself.

'I'd love to have dinner with you,' she said, 'but a date…?'

She studied his face for a moment, saw the teasing gleam in his blue eyes, and knew she had to make her point and make it quickly, before she got herself lost in some kind of relationship that couldn't go anywhere.

'I'm probably ten years older than you—you do realise that?' she said. 'So I don't think our dating is at all appropriate.'

He smiled at her—which she wished he wouldn't do.

'Is there someone else in your life? Or do you worry over what people might think?'

'No and no!' she said. 'I just don't think it's a good idea. And, while there's no one else in *my* life, aren't you forgetting you're still married? You definitely shouldn't be dating!'

'Okay, then,' he said, with a smile and another half-shrug. 'No date, but just dinner together. Do you recommend the café you mentioned?'

It was her turn to shrug. 'Like I said, it's not been open long, and I've been meaning to go, but I haven't got around to it. I *do* hear good things about it.'

He beamed at her, causing so much consternation in her usually reliable body that she scowled at him and said, 'And you can stop smiling like the cat that got the canary, because it is *not* a date!'

'Whatever you say, ma'am,' he said, snapping a half-salute, and leaving the room.

Feeling enormously pleased with himself, Cam retreated to his part of the building, arriving there to find a message from the locum, reminding him that today would be his final day.

Good, he thought, *I'm ready to make this place my own.*

He'd talk to Lauren tonight about tradespeople. The surgery was looking tired, and he wanted to paint the waiting room, bring in some new furniture, and do a complete overhaul of the operating theatre and treatment room.

It was a half-day at the surgery, with the afternoon kept free for farm visits, so with the receptionist and locum both gone he answered the phone when it rang.

An agitated female voice garbled at him, so he caught only a few words, like 'fever', or maybe 'stevia', and something that sounded like 'backpackers'.

She couldn't possibly be calling about feverish backpackers, and his mind spun as he tried to find a possible animal.

'Did you say "alpacas"?' he asked finally.

The woman said, 'Of *course* alpacas—what else would I mean? Stevie's down! Can you come now?'

Stevie? Not fever?

He shook his head, but assured her he could, and she gave him directions to her place further around the lake.

He grabbed the four-wheel drive's keys off the board, and was about to head out when he thought of something.

He dashed through into the sanctuary, where he found Lauren in a store cupboard.

'I don't suppose you know anything about alpacas?' he asked.

She frowned at him, then shook her head. 'Related to camels, aren't they?'

'I *do* know that much!' he said.

'Rye grass,' she said, remembering a long-ago trip to a farm with Henry. 'They can get something called rye grass toxicity.'

'And...?'

'I think they fall over—but whoever owns them will know all that. Just ask the owners. They love to tell vets things. It's like patients and doctors, when the patient has looked up all his symptoms online and discovered he has multi-organism, acute blue spyridium disease.'

Cam laughed. 'Does such a thing exist?' he asked.

Lauren shook her head. 'Not that I know of—but they do find the weirdest things on the Internet, so maybe it does.'

'Okay, I'll ask the owner,' he said. 'See you at seven.'

'You'll be lucky to make it,' she said. 'If the owner is who I think she is, she knows more about alpacas than anyone in the district—if not the world—and loves to educate.'

Cam walked away with a smile on his face. This was the beginning of a new life for him—and in more ways than one. Alpacas, for a start, were not something he'd run across as a London vet.

And Lauren...

He knew his grin had grown wider—but what the hell? Just knowing he'd be seeing her again in a few hours made him...

Made him what?

Want to bounce around a little with excitement?

But that was downright juvenile, so he contented himself with feeling happy.

Very happy.

Extraordinarily happy.

But somewhere below all this delight questions were niggling. It wasn't as if this was his first date since Kate had left him—he'd been quite serious about one young woman he'd taken out—but he hadn't felt like this before.

It was as if Lauren had lit something inside him—brought a dying ember back to life—so the attraction he felt towards her was different in some way. A whole-body kind of experience… which was simply ridiculous even to think about!

He'd be content with happiness…

But then the sane voice inside his brain warned against getting too far ahead of himself, and he picked up the alpacas' address and set out to meet them.

When Lauren had finished her chores, the stock cupboard looked neater than it had in months. Concentrating on the task had helped her to stop herself thinking of the evening ahead.

Thinking *too much* about it, at least.

Pathetic.

She walked swiftly home, aware she needed to shower and change before beginning her afternoon session. Having to hurry helped her not to think about Cam.

Almost not think about Cam…

Although thinking about what decent 'going

out' clothes she had in her wardrobe wasn't exactly *not* thinking about Cam.

She smiled to herself—of course it was thinking about Cam. It was about wanting to look good for him...wanting him to think she looked good.

She shook her head—better than sighing—and reminded herself that she had patients to see...patients who required one hundred per cent of her concentration.

She'd think about Cam later...

Edward Forrest was her first patient—a friend of Henry and her father's, although he'd been a bit younger than them. 'The three old codgers' they'd called themselves, and since Henry had died Edward had become increasingly isolated.

From the moment he rolled into the surgery on his electric buggy and didn't smile at her, she was aware that his gout must be playing up.

She moved forward to greet him and took both his hands in hers. 'Not so good?' she said gently, and he shook his head. 'I'd better have a look,' she said, and knelt to unwrap his heavily bandaged left foot. 'Are you trying to drink more water?' she asked, as she finally revealed his angrily swollen big toe.

Edward huffed and puffed a bit, and finally

admitted that he'd tried to keep drinking water, adding, 'Not that anyone can actually drink two litres of the stuff a day, like that diet sheet you gave me said. There's not enough time in a day, and even with just a few glasses I'm spending half my time peeing.'

Lauren smiled up at him. 'Just keep up with drinking what you can. Forget two litres and try to get into a habit of a glass when you get up, one with your morning cuppa, one at lunch, one in the afternoon and one at dinner time.'

She'd checked his file before he'd come in, and found a note that he'd been growing tomatoes the last time he'd had a flare-up. Growing them and eating them off the bush whenever he was in the garden...

'What have you been eating lately—surely the tomatoes are finished?' she said.

'Prawns,' he announced, in such a tragic voice Lauren had to smile. 'Young Josh came in with a great catch and brought some around, so...well, I had to *eat* them, didn't I?'

'Presumably with a few beers to wash them down?'

'I did not,' he said, sounding most offended. 'You said to cut down on the beer, and prawns go a treat with red wine.'

Lauren closed her eyes. 'Red wine is alcohol too, you know,' she said as she fetched clean dressings. 'You really do have to cut down on *all* alcohol, Edward, if you want to prevent these flare-ups. And the more water you drink to wash the uric acid that builds up in your toe out of your system, the less pain you'll have.'

He muttered something that could have been, 'You've told me that a hundred times,' but Lauren ignored him and wrote him a prescription for the corticosteroid she knew he'd used before.

'Now, remember—take two for three days, then one for three days—'

'Then a half for three days. I know all that,' he told her, as he examined the wrappings she'd placed around his foot. 'That's not too bad,' he said of her work. 'If I keep it wrapped people don't bump into me.'

'Just start taking better care of yourself,' Lauren told him, as she saw him out.

Her next patient was only wanting a new prescription—and, it seemed, a chat about the new vet and the drama up the gully the previous weekend.

'I'd love to be able to chat,' Lauren said, 'but there seem to be more people than usual waiting today, so I'd better crack on.'

The patient departed, and another arrived, and it was life as usual—checking the tonsils of a small child, the ear of a teenager who'd tried a bit of self-piercing and ended up with an infection, and two more older locals mainly wanting info on the new vet.

'Bless their hearts,' Janet said as they locked up, 'It's the biggest excitement in their lives since Henry's death!'

With Janet gone, and nothing to worry about for any of the patients she'd seen, Lauren could no longer *not* think about this evening's outing.

She went up the stairs and through her room to the bathroom.

Shower, wash hair, then think about it!

Towelling her damp hair, she stood in front of her big old wardrobe, peering in at her collection of what she called 'going out' clothes. Not that going out to anywhere in the village required much more than basic decency.

Although, now she thought about it, in summer, when the area had an influx of holiday-makers, some of the teenagers in brief bikini tops and low-slung short shorts barely reached that level.

She returned the towel to the bathroom and combed her hair—still damp, so a darker gold than usual—then went back to the wardrobe. Which was when the absolute stupidity of her behaviour struck her. She'd regressed to her teenage years, when wearing just the right thing had been vitally important.

She should just wear jeans and a top, as the nights were cool.

Except, for the first time in for ever, she had a reason to dress up.

Lauren had to smile, imagining the reaction of the locals if she appeared in one of the lovely outfits she termed her 'wedding' dresses—beautiful clothes she'd bought for special occasions, like friends' weddings. She might look good, but she'd embarrass both herself and Cam, as the village really wasn't a 'dressing up' kind of place.

So, back to jeans and a top. She had a new pair of skinny jeans she'd bought in Riverview recently, and a caramel-coloured knit that she'd bought at the sales up there at the end of last winter. Lightweight, and V-necked, it would be perfect over the black jeans—casually saying *I'm not dressed up*, and yet making her feel good because the jeans were sexy and the top was new.

And, if she was honest, she knew the outfit would definitely suit her!

Unable to remember the last time he'd worried over what to wear made Cam feel jittery.

Jeans and a shirt—nothing easier.

Except he had a small fashionista sitting on his bed.

'You're not going to wear *that*, are you?' Maddie demanded, as he dragged a rugby shirt from the cupboard.

'Why not?' he asked, but he was already putting it back where it had come from.

'You want to make a good 'pression,' Maddie told him.

'I think Lauren's first impression of me, lying on my back in the gully, is probably stamped in her head for ever, so I don't really think she'll notice what I'm wearing.'

'Go for that blue shirt hanging at the end,' she said, pointing to a fairly well-worn corduroy button-down. 'And roll the sleeves up a bit. And don't tuck it in.'

'And just how did you become an expert on menswear?' he asked, surprised by her decided views.

'Uncle Matt always looks good, and that's the sort of stuff he wears.'

With a slow shake of his head Cam realised she was right. In fact, Matt—his oldest friend—had given him the blue shirt years ago, trying to spruce up his suddenly single friend…

Lauren opened the door when she heard the vehicle pull up outside. Too late now to change her top, which she'd decided might be too dressy.

There was so much tension in her body she worried she might shatter at the slightest misstep.

Stupid, really, when all she was doing was going to dinner with a friend.

She breathed deeply, forcing her body to relax, trying to remember what 'normal' felt like.

'You brought the car,' she said, stating the obvious as she pointed to the four-wheel drive. 'It's only half a k, and it's a lovely night; I thought we could walk. If your ankle's all right, that is?'

He bowed and said, 'Then walk we shall! My ankle's fine. I'll leave the car here and take it back later.'

His arm was free of its sling, and with a blue shirt making his eyes seem impossibly bluer, he really was devastatingly good-looking.

And he was studying the front of her house with a slight frown.

'Maddie mentioned the cakes,' he said.

Lauren smiled at him, relaxing. 'Our old housekeeper—Dad's and mine—was the area's champion cake-maker. She made them for weddings, engagements, baptisms—anything and everything. Even made them when there was nothing special on. Mrs Blair is long gone, but I haven't the heart to take down the cake signs—not when in between making cakes she helped make *me*.'

He turned to her and smiled. 'That is such

a nice thing to do,' he said, and the words sent warmth spiralling through her.

Dusk had fallen, but the path around the lake was clear of scrub. He held out his right arm as she joined him, and she tucked her hand into his elbow.

That was only politeness, she told herself, but it brought her body closer to his, and her misgivings about this expedition returned. Given the attraction she felt towards the man, should she really be taking the opportunity to be closer to him?

Yet it felt comfortable...right...

'So, how were the alpacas?' she asked, and he turned to catch the smile that followed her words.

'You *knew* what that woman Celia was like, and did nothing to warn me,' he said, accusation clear in his voice.

'She's a lovely person, you must admit,' Lauren said, still smiling.

'She is—but she's also totally daft about her animals,' Cam responded. 'They're more like children to her—they've all got names, and they *answer* to their names, and they run to her like children do. And can she *talk*! She knew one thousand times more than me about alpacas. But I had a date—yes, I know what you think, but it's easier to just call it a date—and I needed to get away.' He paused, then added, 'It *was* rye grass toxicity—but only one animal. Her beloved Stevie had it, and he'd gone down, and she said he wouldn't get up although he was kicking feebly. She wanted me there to kill him humanely.'

'Oh, dear…poor you,' Lauren said, well aware of how emotional the scene would have been.

'She sat on the ground and held his head while I injected him,' Cam said.

And he sounded so astonished by this behaviour, Lauren had to ask, 'But don't pet owners often hold their pets while they die?'

Cam sighed and stopped walking, turning to look out over the lake for a few minutes.

'Sometimes, yes…but they don't wail in the most broken-hearted manner. I nearly cried myself,' he said. 'For an alpaca I didn't even know!'

Lauren turned to him. 'I'd be more worried about the rye grass than Celia's behaviour. And why only one animal was affected. Did you check the others?'

It was his turn to smile as he turned back towards her. 'If you call "checking" chasing the herd up and down the field to see if any of them fell down, then, yes. Apparently, that's what happens—and who was I to argue.'

'And Stevie?'

'We should walk on or we'll never get there,'

Cam said, steering her back along the path. 'Well, it turned out,' he said after a moment, 'that Celia had bought a bale of feed from a different distributor, but hadn't yet cut the strings. It was in the back of her utility, parked by the fence of Stevie's pen, and he'd been putting his head over and munching on it. Celia's certain she has no rye grass in any of her fields, so thinks it must be in the new feed.'

'She'll soon sort it out,' Lauren said, walking more slowly as they approached the village.

Perhaps they should have driven, she thought. And kind of sneaked in…?

She felt embarrassed that she'd even thought of it.

Not that it would have made the slightest difference, whatever they'd done. They'd be seen at dinner and it would be all over the local community within hours. Memories of the talk there'd been way back when David had disappeared from her life surfaced briefly, and she had to remind herself that she'd ignored it then and could do so again.

Not that one dinner out would start much gossip…would it?

She glanced at her companion, but he was looking out over the lake again, taking in the picturesque beauty of the trawlers moored at the end of the jetty, the moon just rising behind them.

'It *is* a beautiful place,' he said quietly, and she felt a rush of pleasure at this compliment to her home.

They continued in silence. Cam was pleased just to take in the beauty of the place, especially with Lauren by his side. He sensed a tension in her, and guessed that, at the moment, it was more to do with local gossip than their age difference.

He'd already heard from many of the people he'd met through work how wonderful she was—not only as a doctor, but with her volunteer work—and he knew that the gossip wouldn't harm her. Embarrass her, maybe, but she was held in such high esteem in the town it couldn't damage her.

Should he tell her that?

Would it ease her tension? Relax her back into the laughing, teasing, wonderful woman he was beginning to know?

Or *was* her tension to do with the age thing... silly though that seemed to him?

Unable to reach any conclusion, he looked around and realised they'd reached their destination.

CHAPTER FIVE

PARADISE EATERY the sign proclaimed. There were tiny fairy lights strung along the building's guttering and threaded through the potted trees on either side of the front door.

Lauren was already being greeted by the woman at the front counter, and Cam followed the two women to a table.

'Cam is my new neighbour, in Henry's place,' Lauren said. 'Campbell Grahame, meet Nell Wright—owner of this establishment.'

Nell shook his hand, welcoming him, and added, 'You're the new vet, aren't you?'

'I am—and I've taken over completely now the locum's gone. He seems to think I've learned all I need to know, but I rather doubt that.'

'Well, I've only got a tortoise, so I probably won't be calling on you professionally,' Nell said. 'I'll get you both a menu.'

She returned with menus and an offer of drinks.

'What would you like?' he asked Lauren.

'A light beer, please, Nell,' she said, and Cam followed suit, rather pleased he wasn't going to have to consult a list of wines. He didn't know if the Australian wines he'd consumed back home went by the same names in their home country.

Nell departed and he turned towards Lauren, seeing in the room's soft light how the sweater she was wearing set off her golden-coloured hair and emphasised her dark brown eyes.

She was beautiful—but he knew she wouldn't thank him for saying so.

Work conversations would probably be easier. Which reminded him...

'I don't suppose you know anything about pregnancy testing alpacas, do you?'

She laughed with delight, shaking her head at the same time.

'Inappropriate dinner table conversation?' he suggested, and she clearly took pity on him and reached out to pat his hand where it lay on the table.

'No, it just surprised me,' she said. 'But sadly I don't—I can't be any help at all!' She frowned for a moment, then added, 'Wouldn't it be much the same as testing cows? Or maybe sheep?'

His turn to laugh. 'Lauren, I'm a city vet— straight from London to this totally alien environment, where I have to treat burnt koalas, dying alpacas, and heaven only knows what next. Yes, we did cover large animals at vet school—even elephants—but I probably didn't take a lot of notice as I knew I wanted to be a city vet.'

'Oh!' she said, suddenly grave. 'So did you *want* to move here, or just feel obliged to because of Henry leaving the place to you? Couldn't you have sold it?'

She sounded concerned for him, and he'd have liked to pat *her* hand in return, but both of them had disappeared beneath the table.

'We were delighted to move here—Maddie especially, and for me it was a tremendous gift. My very own practice. In the place I'd heard so much about from Uncle Henry's letters. I couldn't have been happier. But I assumed it would still be mainly domestic pets—which, from the study I've done of Henry's books, it seems to be.'

'Just the odd alpaca thrown in?' Lauren teased.

He grinned at her, unsure if the delight he was feeling was purely to do with Lauren, or simply because he was out with an attractive woman for the first time in what seemed like ages.

Looking at the smiling woman across the table, he knew it was Lauren making him feel so good. In fact, he doubted any other woman would have made him feel the same.

He was considering telling her how great she

looked, when she glanced up from the menu she was studying and said, 'I remember going around with Henry when I was a teenager to preg-test sheep. He used a portable ultrasound, I think at about forty days after they'd been run with the rams, but I could be wrong about the timing.'

'I'll have to ultrasound an alpaca? A small herd of alpacas?' he asked, thinking of the rather weird, long-legged and long-necked animals.

'You do have a portable one, I imagine?'

'Of course,' he said, taking a gulp of his beer in an effort to stabilise his whirling thoughts.

How had they gone from him telling her how good she looked—even if only in his thoughts—to ultra-sounding herd animals?

It was probably a good thing, he decided, given this outing wasn't a date. But it *had* told him one thing—he had to get on to Kate and insist she sign the divorce papers she'd been sitting on for months. Well, maybe not insist—because he lived with the fear that if he pushed too hard she'd take the matter to court and put his custody of Maddie in jeopardy.

He focussed his attention back on Lauren and realised she was still talking about alpacas.

'Celia will handle it all,' she assured him, and then turned to the waiter. 'I'll have the prawn pasta, please, and a small salad on the side.'

Totally discombobulated, he shook his head

and looked at his own menu. 'Eye fillet, medium rare,' he said, 'and a side of vegetables, please.'

The waiter bustled away, and Lauren smiled at him across the table.

'I bet "vegetables" here mean a half a plate of chips and some sprouts and carrot and broccoli in a little bowl because they don't fit on the plate.'

'And *what* is wrong with steak and chips?' he demanded.

She grinned at him. 'Not a thing to a long, slim beanpole like you. You can carry a bit of extra weight. But me... Although I'm tall, any weight I put on goes straight to my belly or my butt, leaving my arms and legs as thin as twigs.'

He smiled at her. 'Fishing for compliments? I can't see your legs or arms, but you look just stunning—and I imagine your life is far too busy for you to be putting on weight.'

She smiled and drank a little more beer—embarrassed, he thought, but pleased as well.

What on earth was she doing, going out with this man? Date or not, it felt so comfortable, so enjoyable, she'd be hard pushed to say no should he ask her again.

But he was married, and there was the difference in their ages...

And yet...

'You know,' she said, because he deserved honesty, 'I can't remember when I last had a normal conversation with another adult. I mean, I see adult patients every day, and the people at the sanctuary as well—even the other SES workers at training days and meetings—but, honestly, it's not the same. It's just chat.'

She studied his face, which told her nothing, then pushed on.

'It's wonderful,' she said, 'and I'm glad you asked me.'

His smile lit up his face to such a degree that she wondered if she'd said the wrong thing... given him the impression that she was enjoying their—dreaded word—*date*!

But of course she *was*.

'So, we'll have to do it again,' he said, right on cue. 'Maybe try the golf club? Or go up to the city to somewhere fancy.'

It's not a date, she wanted to remind him. But then she thought, *Why the hell not?* Why shouldn't she get out and have a bit of fun? It had been so long she'd almost forgotten the pleasure of pleasant, undemanding company.

Their meals had arrived while she was considering these astounding revelations, and without a second thought she reached out and pinched a chip from his plate.

He lifted the plate and brought it closer to her,

obviously intending to push some chips onto her side plate.

'Have some more,' he said, but she waved the offer away.

'That was me reverting to childhood,' she explained. 'Whenever I went out to dinner with Edward, Henry and my father, I'd pinch chips from their plates.'

'What about your mother?' he asked.

She smiled and took a quick breath. 'I never knew her. She was diagnosed with breast cancer while she was pregnant with me and she refused to have an abortion, or any treatment, in case it interfered with the pregnancy. She died soon after I was born.'

He shook his head, such disbelief on his face that she knew he was thinking about the sacrifice her mother had made—it was the same thought that had kept her on track all through her life.

'How on earth did your father manage?' he asked.

Lauren smiled. 'Same way you did with Maddie after your wife left. People just do the best they can. Dad had Henry and Edward too. Henry was a bit older, and had never married, but he was the prop that kept my father going. Between the three of them, and my mother's mother, who came for a few days whenever she could, I think they did a pretty good job.'

Cam looked up from the steak he was cutting and smiled at her. 'I think they did an excellent job.'

'Ah, but you didn't think that the day I rescued you,' she reminded him, and he laughed.

'I was so cranky with myself for flying that darned machine I couldn't think straight,' he said, and smiled at her. 'I do apologise—again. You were wonderful. *Are* wonderful.'

Embarrassed by his praise, Lauren picked the prawns out of her pasta—which was delicious. Suddenly she was not very hungry. But she needed something fiddly to do to stop her thinking about Cam's praise.

Was he just a flirt, or was he fancying himself in love with her?

Surely not the latter. They barely knew each other!

But something in his eyes when he'd told her she was wonderful had had the glow of—what?

The same attraction she was feeling towards him?

The same feeling that there was some kind of electric current flashing between them…?

They finished the meal with a soft, gooey apple and rhubarb crumble and ice-cream, after which

Lauren declared she was very glad they'd walked as they could walk off some of it on the way home.

Then they argued about the bill. Cam insisted he'd asked her out, and intended to pay; Lauren countering that with her 'not a date' stance.

'I'll pay next time,' she told him, after he'd insisted, and after it had become clear that arguing further would cause a disturbance in the busy restaurant.

'So, there'll be a next time?' he teased as he tucked her hand into the crook of his elbow again and eased her closer to his body.

'How can I say no,' she grumbled, 'when it was the best time I've had in ages?'

'How many ages?' he asked.

And she knew he really wanted to know.

She sighed.

Knew she should explain…

'I studied in Sydney, and did my GP training placements down there, then came home for a holiday with Dad. I hadn't seen him for a while, although we'd talked on the phone, and I suppose I must have been a little worried about him, because I told David, my fiancé, that I might have to stay a while.'

'And "a while" turned into for ever?' Cam asked, and slid his arm around her shoulder in a comforting way.

She nodded. 'It was soon evident that my dad wasn't managing—he was forgetting things, losing words, and his mind was wandering when he should have been working. Henry was aware of it, and he was the one who told me Dad had been losing more than words—he'd been losing patients to other doctors. I knew I'd have to take over completely. I brought in a young man to take care of Dad when I was working—to take him for walks in the bush, which he loved, or out on Henry's boat…did you know you have a boat? And I took over the practice, getting in help when I needed, and became Dad's primary carer.'

'And David?'

Lauren stopped walking and turned to Cam. 'David couldn't handle it—couldn't understand that I wouldn't walk away from the man who'd made me what I was. You're bringing up a daughter—you must know the limits it places on your own life. Dad had done that for me.' She was silent for a moment before adding, 'But David's life was in Sydney, working his way through an orthopaedic specialty—he had no time for a long-distance romance.'

She paused, turned to walk again.

'I think I was more upset about my poor choice of life partner than the actual break-up. I threw my engagement ring in the lake—which upset him far more than his desertion upset me. He seemed to think I should have given it back for his next fiancée.'

'Getting even?' Cam said, and Lauren smiled at him.

'More getting rid of the past.'

They walked on again, and Lauren was suddenly conscious of the fact she'd just told Cam more than she'd ever told anyone. For years she'd guarded her heart against the hurt David's rejection had caused. She'd kept it tucked away, pretending to understand and not be unduly bothered—mainly to protect her father from feeling guilty that she'd given up so much for him, back in the early days when he'd have understood.

But now…?

To talk about it…and to Cam of all people…

For whatever reason, she'd opened herself up in a way that made her feel vulnerable, so when their pace slowed, and Cam turned her towards him, she didn't resist, but nestled in his arms and raised her head for the kiss she knew was coming.

You're just seeking comfort, her head told her, but her response to his kiss was more than just comfort.

It was hunger—as raw and needy as she had ever felt.

But this was Cam—her neighbour—someone she was likely to see nearly every day. And even as his response sent her heart into overdrive, and long-forgotten sensations stirred her body, the warnings in her head grew more strident.

How would she feel in the morning, when all the doubts she had about a relationship with Cam would come surging back? His age, his marital status, her fear of being hurt again… And the unspoken one—the fear of what might lie ahead of her…the shadow of her father's illness.

She eased away, dropped her head so his lips kissed her forehead. 'It's too much of a muddle,' she whispered. 'Too hard for me to think about—to think clearly at all.'

He drew her close again and nuzzled her neck. 'Were you always this sensible? Have you always analysed every move you make?'

She couldn't think with that nuzzling going on, making desire burn hotter.

She eased away again. 'I think I probably have,' she said, and this time she stepped away and turned resolutely towards her house. 'It wasn't that Dad and Henry ever set rules for me. But I was always conscious of not wanting them to—well, to be disappointed in me, I suppose. I was conscious, as I grew older, that they'd probably given up a lot of their own pursuits to bring me up.'

Cam gave her a one-armed hug. 'So,' he said, with amusement in his voice, 'Great-Uncle Henry not only left me a house, a veterinary practice, an animal sanctuary and a flying machine, but also a woman of principle! Is that it?'

She smiled at him. 'Kind of...' she said. 'I just don't know...' She sighed. 'I don't *get* muddled,' she added, a little later. But it sounded feeble even in her own mind. 'This is just totally beyond anything I've ever imagined, and I don't know how to *begin* to think about it.'

She studied his face.

'Let's walk,' she said, and took his hand to lead him on along the path to their homes.

Cam didn't know how to think about it, either. This woman was unlike anyone he'd ever known.

Was it that she was so principled?

Yes, but he'd known plenty of other principled people—his own parents, for a start—and he rather hoped it was a trait he had himself.

So it was something else that made Lauren different—and even more attractive than just the physical pull she had on him.

She'd stopped walking, pausing to look out at the lake, and he studied her, so beautiful in the moonlight, with the silvered lake behind her, the silence of the bush around them.

'I think you might just have bewitched me,' he said. 'Because all I can think about is how soon we can do this again.' He drew her closer and kissed her chastely on the lips. 'Friends?' he asked as he drew away.

She smiled at him. 'Friends!' she whispered, and then turned to take the track to her house, leaving him to go on to his vehicle, shaking his head at the way a simple dinner out had grown into such a muddle.

It really was the only word.

His fault, of course. Wanting to rush headlong into things the way he had with the ultralight.

He gave a huff of laughter.

Comparing Lauren to an ultralight?

No way!

Lauren went into the house, closed the door and leaned against it. She stayed upright this time—behaving like the adult she was. But the contact with Cam had shaken her—and not only physically. It had affected her perception of who she was.

She had always seen herself as a strong, independent woman. And in recent years her life balance of work, volunteering, exercise and get-togethers with friends had been all she'd needed or wanted. She *liked* the solitariness of her life—

the need to please only herself in choosing what to do, what to eat, what holidays to plan.

She knew it came from being a solitary child, happy making up her own games in the bush around the house, too far from the village and the school for other children to be around. At boarding school for her senior years she'd become friends with others like her—young people from distant places who went back home when each term was finished.

Then at university, right there in the same college as her, had been David, and the two of them had become a couple—bringing a new type of isolation with her friend and lover…being a couple in the midst of singles.

So why change the habits of a lifetime and get involved with the man next door? The *young* man next door…

Although, apart from the ultralight adventure, he didn't come across as young. Probably being left to bring up a small daughter alone had matured him beyond his years.

With a sigh—it was becoming a habit, this sighing—she slid into her normal routine, checking the downstairs doors were all locked before climbing up to her room, where she walked to the open window and leant on the sill to stare out at the night.

Was Cam looking out at the lake too?

Silly thought. She really had to stop thinking about it—about him.

The melody of the mobile phone in her pocket startled her. Not because she never had night call-outs, but because she'd been so lost in her own thoughts.

'I hoped you were still up.' Cam's voice was urgent. 'It's a dog—left on my front step, wrapped in a blanket. He's badly injured and I need help if I'm going to save him. Could you come?'

'Of course.' It was the only answer. Aware that his veterinary nurse lived close to Riverview, she realised why he'd rung her.

She quickly pulled off her good sweater and pulled on a T-shirt. She'd grab a jacket from the rack near the front door—and shoes. Her ankle-height wellies were by the front door, too. She'd wear those.

Within minutes she was at Cam's place, and saw the lights were on in his veterinary rooms. She made her way there, going in through the open door, closing it behind her.

'Cam?' she called.

'In here—the surgery. You know it?'

Indeed, she did. She'd loved watching Henry with the animals.

Cam's 'going out' clothes were covered with a green gown, and as she walked in he pulled down the cloth mask that covered his mouth and nose.

'I've put a gown out on the bench for you, and a mask and gloves with it,' he said, then returned his mask to its place and his attention to his patient.

He glanced up when Lauren joined him at the table, his blue eyes angry and intent. 'I think he's been injured in illegal dog-fighting,' he said, barely taking his eyes off the animal as he probed the gashes and tears in the poor dog's skin and muscle.

'I thought that had been snuffed out—illegal dog fighting,' she said. 'I haven't heard of any in the area—although I suppose I don't go to places where I might hear.'

He glanced up at her again. 'I think it just goes further underground when the authorities try to stop it,' he said, and she could hear the bitter anger in his voice. 'This is a fairly isolated area—I imagine that out beyond the lake and the village there are plenty of sheds the organisers can use...and possibly some own a shed or two as well as dogs.'

'What can I do to help?' Lauren asked, and he looked up from his examination of the injured dog as if surprised to see that she was there.

'I've mixed some disinfectant in that bowl over there. If you could take a cloth from that pile and try to clean him up a bit… Later we'll need antibacterial solution to clean out the wounds, but for now I just need to see the extent of the damage.'

Cam was swabbing wounds on the animal's head, so she began at the other end, wiping off mud and blood and who knew what from the animal's skin.

'He's got old scars and some bruising,' Lauren said, cleaning his belly and seeing a clear boot mark.

'The owners treat them badly—starve them, beat them…anything to make them angry enough to fight.' His voice was hard with a fury that seemed to burn in him.

'Oh, Cam…' she whispered, as the thought of what this animal had been through hit her. 'There are some quite deep bite marks here on the side of his shoulder,' she said, as she worked her way from the tail up. 'And from the look of that tear on his face that you're swabbing, he's been badly mauled.' She paused, then asked quietly, 'Have you thought of euthanising?'

'No way.'

The words were ground out from between gritted teeth.

'I am going to get this guy back on his feet and then talk to the police about the bastards who did this to him. They must have some inkling that this is happening, and they're the ones who need to stop it. This is illegal, and the penalties are harsh, but they're so secret, these fights, that the venues change—perhaps even week to week. And that means the law doesn't have the time or the manpower to pursue them—at least, not in the UK.'

'And you do?' she murmured, feeling rather fearful that he was angry enough to put himself in danger. She knew enough about dog fighting to know that a lot of people made money out of it.

'I'll make a fuss,' he growled. 'That's the least I can do. Now, if you'll help me turn him, we'll clean up the other side and get started on repairs.'

But as they turned the dog they saw the pool of blood, and the torn blood vessel that had leaked it.

'Damn—I thought I'd checked that!' Cam muttered. 'I'll clean it up and suture the leaking blood vessel before we do any more.'

He was holding the seeping vessel with his fingers, peering around helplessly.

'Look,' Lauren said, 'you know where to put your hands on everything you need. I'll hold that while you set up.'

He glanced at her with a grateful smile and stepped aside so she could take his place. Her fingers slid over his to grasp the blood vessel, and his closeness as they swapped brought a flash of the warmth she'd felt earlier.

Idiot, she told herself. *We have a life to save here, so get with the programme.*

Working with Cam was special, in a challenging kind of way. She just hoped his very real anger at the practice of dog fighting wouldn't lead him into trouble.

Trouble?

She barely knew this man, but she instinctively felt that 'trouble' might be his middle name.

His Great-Uncle Henry had had a streak of bravado a mile wide—he'd always been willing to have a go at anything, no matter how impossible!

Fifteen minutes later, with the bleeder sutured and the dog relatively clean, they could see the extent of the damage.

'Okay,' Cam said, 'now for some surgery. You ever been a surgery nurse?'

She smiled at him. 'Not as such. But I did do a surgical rotation during training, and a couple more in my intern years, so if you keep the orders simple I should be able to manage.'

Cam insisted they both gowned up in fresh gear—and even allowed her to help him on with his gloves after he'd washed his hands with the particular care of a surgeon. She followed him at the basin, washing her hands and pulling on new gloves and mask.

He checked their patient's heart-rate and pulse, shaking his head at the fact that an animal so badly injured should still be not only hanging in, but hanging in strongly.

'Nothing like the will to live, is there?' he said to Lauren, the blue eyes above his mask shining with admiration for the plucky animal.

And, even in this fairly critical conversation, Lauren felt her knees go wobbly at the gleam in his eyes.

Concentrate, she told herself.

Cam paid attention to the facial injuries first, leaving the deep bite marks behind the dog's ear untended.

'That's where the worst infection is likely to be,' he said. 'I've flushed them out as much as possible, and I'll leave them open so I can keep an eye on them.'

He moved a portable X-ray screen and positioned it above the left front leg, which was badly mutilated, but the X-ray, when they both peered at it on the little office screen, showed no breaks to the bones, although the shoulder tendons were badly torn.

It was two hours before Cam was finally satisfied that he'd done all he could for the dog at the moment, and the animal was swathed in bandages.

'How will you keep him quiet enough to allow the wounds to heal?' Lauren asked, scratching at a small patch of unbandaged skin on the dog's back.

'With so much damage, I'll sedate him for twelve hours,' Cam said. 'I just hope that when it wears off he feels bad enough not to want to move. I don't want to keep him in a crate, which would be the obvious answer. He was probably kept in one most of this life, and he'll be terrified. The poor chap is traumatised...'

He hesitated, his eyes on the dog, his hand absently fondling the animal's head.

'I'll put him in a kennel out in one of the runs,' he decided finally. 'They're all empty at the moment, apart from one very pregnant cat. I'll keep them well apart and I'll just close off the open run so he can't get out into the rather patchy grass.'

But Lauren was barely listening. 'You think he's been kept in a crate?' she whispered, her heart aching at the thought of this dog's life. On impulse, she added, 'Can I have him when he's better? I have a patient who really needs a dog, and I've told him I'll find one. This fellow can come and convalesce with me, and I'll introduce him to Mr Richards as soon as he's up and about again—the dog, not Mr Richards. And if he doesn't want him, I'll keep him. My last dog died two years ago, and I haven't felt up to replacing him before now.'

'We'll have to see,' Cam said, sounding so exhausted that Lauren suddenly realised how late it was—close to three in the morning.

'I should go,' she said. 'And, no, you definitely don't need to walk me home.' She put her hands on his shoulders and looked deep into his tired eyes. 'I'll be fine,' she said, and won an exhausted smile. 'You go to bed.'

'All alone?' he managed.

She gave him a little shake. 'As if you're fit for anything else...'

She kissed his cheek and stepped away from him, but he caught her hand.

'I want to come with you.'

She squeezed his fingers, then disentangled them. 'Look,' she said, touching his shoulder, 'if you're really worried I'll take Henry's old bike and be home in no time.'

His smile was a weak effort.

She kissed him again, quickly on the lips, then turned him towards the stairs, and said, 'Go to bed! Now!'

Only after he'd settled the dog in a bed in one of the kennels, and cleaned up most of the mess, did he follow her orders.

She didn't take the bike, preferring a quiet walk home along the path she knew so well. The peacefulness of it helped the tension of the operation—of Cam—to slowly subside.

When she did get home, she showered, fell into bed, and was still asleep when Janet arrived for work, calling up the stairs to her that there were patients waiting!

Cam was awoken by a small hand tugging at his arm.

'Daddy, there's a dog in one of the kennels all over bandages! He looks sad and I think he's hungry.'

Cam opened his eyes and peered blearily at his daughter. 'What were you doing out at the kennels?' he asked.

Maddie smiled at him. 'I went to visit the cat. Madge came with me, with the food. No kittens yet, but she's so big they must be coming soon!'

He closed his eyes, aware that he needed to get up, showered, dressed and fed, and to be ready for any patient that might come in.

'Be a love and slip downstairs and ask Madge if she'll make me some coffee. Tell her to use Henry's old filter machine—I'll need more than one cup.'

'But what about the dog?' Maddie asked, edging backwards towards the door.

'Later,' he said. 'Now, go!'

With his first coffee in hand, he walked out to the kennels, where the dog lay quietly, stiff with tension in spite of the sedation.

Cam squatted beside him. 'Hello, old boy,' he said gently. 'You'll be feeling a bit rough, but we'll soon get you well.'

He moved the bowl of clean water closer, talking all the while, hoping his tone would tell the dog that he was safe.

'I'll be back later,' he said, and hurried back to his rooms, where a parrot who needed his toenails clipped was waiting for him, and Madge was sitting at the reception desk where his nurse usually sat.

'She went off with the locum,' Madge murmured to him as he carried his patient into the treatment room. 'She left a note, and an address for you to send on any mail and wages, if they're due.'

Oh, great, he thought. But his attention was on the bird, who was eyeing him closely, as if deciding where best to nip him.

'He's really gentle, and very old, so he won't bite,' his owner said.

Wrong.

One look at the clippers and the bird let out an indignant squawk and nipped him sharply on the thumb.

But the job was soon done, the thumb bandaged, and his next patient—a constipated poodle—had arrived.

Somehow he got through the morning, and he had finally closed the door, aware that he should be writing up all the notes his nurse would normally do, but craving a small nap instead, when Lauren arrived.

'I thought I'd sit with the dog for a while... just talking to him.'

'Forget the dog—you're an answer to a prayer.' He paused then added, 'No, don't forget the dog. I have to look at him anyway, and if you've the time to talk quietly to him that would be excellent, but first of all do you know anyone who'd like a kitten, or a job as a veterinary nurse?'

It said a lot for Lauren's equanimity that, although she smiled, she honed in on the immediate problem.

'Don't vet nurses need special training?' she asked.

'Usually,' he said, 'but if I can't get a qualified one straight away, even just someone to sit at the desk would do...'

He looked so uptight—this usually ultra-casual man—that she immediately crossed to his desk and lifted the phone.

'The agency who supplies temps when my

nurse or receptionist go on leave might know someone,' she explained as she waited on hold. 'Some don't last long because we're an hour's drive down from Riverview, and they don't like the commute, and if they rent down here they miss the city's social life.'

The phone was finally answered at the agency and Lauren asked about trained veterinary nurses. The woman she spoke to was someone she knew, who assured her there was a young woman living on the lake somewhere who was fully trained.

'She'll get back to me,' Lauren reported to Cam, when the conversation had finished, and explained to him that one might be available locally. 'Actually, she'll probably phone you, as I rang from your number.'

He just stared at her, as if stunned that she'd made it sound so easy.

'So, the dog…?' Lauren said, bringing him back to the reason for her visit. 'How is he? May I go and talk to him?'

'What about the kittens?' he said.

Lauren shook her head at his persistence. 'Are they even born yet?' she asked, and he shook his head in turn. 'Then wait until they are, then wait again until they're about a week old and totally furry and adorable, tumbling over each other. Then take some pictures and put them up in the

shops in the village—they'll be gone in no time.'
She hesitated before adding, 'You might have
to promise to spay them when it's time, but that
shouldn't be a bother.'

He grinned at her. 'Thanks a bunch,' he said.

But she'd stopped listening, her thoughts back
on the dog. 'So, can I sit with the dog?'

Cam frowned, obviously weighing up some
objections. 'You'll need to be careful,' he said.
'He's probably been abused all his life, and he'll
see all people as abusers, so he might try to get
in first with a snap or a bite.'

Lauren smiled at him. 'He's so trussed up, I
doubt he can do me much harm,' she said.

But Cam still looked worried. 'There's another
thing...' he said, and she waited.

And waited!

'You might get too close to him,' he finally
admitted, 'and that might not be good for you
or him.'

'Why ever not?' Lauren demanded. 'I've already told you I know someone who'll take him
when he's better.'

'That's as may be,' Cam said, clearly still worried. 'But he could turn out to be too aggressive, even dangerous, and he might have to be
put down anyway.'

'No way!' Lauren told him. 'Don't even *think*

about that until we see what a little kindness and friendship might do for him.'

She could see Cam was unconvinced, and she knew that he was operating, as she was, on not enough sleep.

'Just let me spend some time with him,' she added. 'I'll be very careful.'

She could tell he was about to agree, but would insist on accompanying her.

'I'll be fine, and I think he'll be better with one person rather than two,' she said, touching him on the arm. 'Just tell me the code for the gate and then go have a sleep.'

He did so reluctantly, and as soon as she'd repeated the numbers she left his rooms and headed for the kennels.

She was pleased, when she considered it, to be out of Cam's presence. Away from the unsettling feelings he caused her...from the urge to move close to him, to—

Don't even go there, she told herself.

What with one thing and another, there'd been far too much togetherness between them lately— and for all the strange sensations it was causing in her body it was feeling far too comfortable.

Almost normal...

CHAPTER SIX

HER AFTERNOON PATIENTS WERE, again, mainly people needing new prescriptions and wanting to know just what was going on with their long-term single doctor.

Like in any small country town—or village, really—anyone new was newsworthy, and for a male newcomer to be seen out and about with the local spinster... Well, she'd known it would start the tongues wagging...

'They say he's a nice man, the new vet,' one woman said. 'Did his wife die?' she asked.

Which brought up something Lauren really didn't want to think about.

She avoided answering the question with a blood pressure check, and went on to ask about her patient's grandchildren—always a welcome topic.

But his marital status was questioned again by her last patient, a schoolteacher pretending interest in Maddie but really after gossip.

Lauren avoided that too, by asking about the woman's eldest, who was up in Riverview at university. Doing well, apparently.

'It's all they're talking about,' Janet said to her when she'd shown the final patient out. 'It's because you went out to dinner with him—now everyone knows.'

'Knows what?' Lauren demanded, far too abruptly, because she knew that Janet would always be thinking of Lauren's interests.

'You know what people are like,' Janet said. 'And anyone new gets talked about. So you'll have to accept a little gossip about yourself and the new vet, even if it was only a very casual dinner.'

'It *was*!' Lauren snorted, then realised she was too tired to be thinking clearly. 'I'm sorry I snapped, Janet,' she said. 'I didn't get much sleep last night—and, no, it's not what you're thinking, you wretch.'

She explained about the dog.

But the marital status questions stayed with her as she went through to her kitchen and made a sandwich, then gathered a few scraps of meat she had in the refrigerator to take over to the dog. She'd wrap her sandwich and take it over there— they would eat together, her and the dog...

Getting back to Cam... He *was* married, and she had to remember that. People who left to 'find themselves' could easily come back. And his wife had been a good mother—Cam had told her that.

Although Lauren felt she'd managed perfectly well without a mother, she did remember times, particularly in her teens, when she'd have loved to have had a mother to talk to, to tell her things... To comfort her when things—boys, more often than not—were disturbing or upsetting her teenage self.

Her consideration of this stayed with her on her walk across to his house and around to the kennels, where she keyed in the gate code and made her way carefully to the injured dog's run.

She spoke softly to him as she approached the gloom of the kennel in the dusk, and wondered if there'd be a light. Did injured dogs need night lights?

'Hello, old boy,' she said, as she came quietly into the shelter.

'Not so much of the "old", thank you,' a deep voice said, and she let out a cry of what she hoped hadn't sounded like fear.

'What on earth are you doing here?' she demanded.

'He's my patient,' Cam said.

But the lack of sleep, concern about the dog, and the muddle she was in over her feelings for this man all crashed down on her and she slumped onto the floor, head bent, as her eyes started leaking tears.

'Hey…' Cam said, standing up and moving so he could sit beside her and put his arm around her. 'I gave you a fright. I'm sorry.'

He pulled her close against his body and she felt his lips pressing kisses on her hair.

'This is stupid,' she finally managed to mutter. 'I never cry.'

He held her closer, so his body warmed her, and just for a minute or two she relaxed against him, nestled into him.

'It's lack of sleep,' she said against his chest. 'And the dog.'

Having produced two more or less sensible sentences, she knew she should ease away— ease out of those arms that held her, away from the security that was something she'd never known…never felt before.

Had she been lonelier than she'd thought? Was that why Cam's arms were so comforting?

She didn't think so—had never felt that. So it must be Cam's arms in particular that were producing these wonderful sensations…

This was dangerous!

But although the word was like a red light, flashing in her brain, she let him hold her, finally lifting her head for the kiss she was sure they both wanted.

The kiss was warm and comforting, but there was more than that to it. Sensuality and desire caused a physical ache deep inside her—a yearning for something she could barely understand.

She finally eased away from him, dug a handkerchief out of her jeans and cleaned up the remnants of her silly tears.

Back in control.

Almost…

Deep breath, and then sensible conversation.

'I've a sandwich, if you'd like to share, and I brought a few scraps of ham for the dog, if that's okay and if he wants it.'

She knew she was yammering on so that she didn't have to think—or, worse, talk about what had just happened—but Cam accepted half her sandwich and agreed that the dog might like the ham.

He sounded so cool and in control. She still felt confused about her weakness, and found herself feeding bits of sandwich to the dog, so she didn't have to think about the man who'd held her in his arms and somehow managed to kiss her body back to life.

'Well, he's certainly well enough to eat,' Cam said, definitely in control. 'I'll feed him mine as well, if you don't mind?'

'Go for it,' Lauren managed, but her voice was husky and a trifle wobbly.

Cam pulled her close again. 'Come on,' he said, 'I'll walk you home. We'll have some tea and toast—if you've any bread left after the sandwiches.'

'I've always got spare bread in my freezer,' Lauren said, deciding it was time to take control of the situation.

'I was almost sure you would,' he said, and she could hear the smile in his voice.

In spite of all the reasons she could list for *not* getting involved with this man, she knew she wanted nothing more than for him to walk her home, his arm around her shoulders, his body close to hers…

They did have tea and toast—but much later.

Cam was more or less dressed—his T-shirt was on inside out—and Lauren was in her faded old dressing gown, cuddly and familiar.

'I shouldn't have let that happen,' she said, her face still flushed from their lovemaking.

'And why is that, oh, wise one?' Cam teased.

She frowned at him. 'You know very well—there are dozens of reasons.'

'Like?' he prompted.

Again that smile was in his voice, and her body trembled.

Get a grip, she told herself.

'Gossip,' she said, 'which won't bother me,

but might be hard for Madge to listen to, and it could hurt Maddie too.'

'Not the dog?' he teased, but she shook her head.

'It's not a joke,' she said. 'This community might be spread out about the lake but it's small, and there's nothing a small community likes better than some fresh gossip.'

'Would it hurt *you*?' he asked, not joking now, and his blue eyes looked at her so tenderly she had to bite back tears.

Bloody hell. Hadn't she cried enough for one day?

'No,' she said. 'I've been here so long I'm just part of the furniture. Although...' She thought about it, and finally admitted, '*Because* I have been here so long, it might be even more startling—juicier.'

She wasn't going to sigh again.

No tears and no sighing.

'And then there's your age,' she said bluntly. 'Lakesiders are fairly conventional people. Cradle-snatching will come up somewhere along the line.'

'Not if we got married,' he said.

And this time she wanted to sigh and cry at the same time.

'Aren't you already married?'

She was watching him closely, wanting to

read his reaction. She didn't expect the smile that came.

'I *am* trying to get unmarried,' he said. 'In fact, one of the reasons I was so delighted to move out here was because my wife is in Australia and I thought it would be easier to push her to sign divorce papers from here.'

Lauren was telling herself she shouldn't feel pleased about this when he floored her completely.

'I think I was smitten the first time I saw you—or very soon after—so it seems natural to think of marriage.'

'*Smitten?* What do you mean "smitten"? And if it's what I think it means it's a passing thing, nothing more, and certainly not a basis for marriage—which isn't possible anyway, given where we're at!'

She folded her arms as she finished this rant, and glared at him—not that her glare had the slightest effect. In fact, it seemed to encourage him, because he left his stool on the other side of the breakfast bar and came to put his arm around her, pulling her to her feet and kissing her so passionately on the lips that her bones began to melt.

Dear heaven, what was she supposed to do?

Let him carry her into the sitting room?

Let him slip off her robe?

Let him kiss his way down from her mouth to her neck, to her breast?

Yes.

So she let him tease and tantalise her, until she joined in the teasing, the kissing, the movement of their bodies as they came together...

He tipped her so she was on top of him, sliding into her, his hands on her breasts making her moan as he moved and cry out as she climaxed, his matching groan of satisfaction sweet in her ears.

CHAPTER SEVEN

FOR THE SECOND morning in a row she was woken by Janet arriving for work, and as she flung herself out of bed she called down to her, asking her to please put on toast, and the kettle. She walked into the bathroom. She could feel him still…his skin against hers, the scent of him in the air around her.

Her body flushed with heat just thinking about it and she dived into the shower, hoping that common sense would soon return, and that she'd at least outwardly look normal and composed.

Fortunately, the morning passed smoothly enough, the only surprise arrival being Madge, towing a reluctant Maddie along behind her.

'She's starting school next week and I'm told she needs some final vaccination, before she goes. I've got her record book from London, so you can see what she's had.'

She passed a small booklet to Lauren, who

checked through the vaccinations Maddie had already received.

'There's not one for meningococcal here,' she said to Madge. 'They're usually given to under-twos and fifteen-to-nineteen-year-olds, because those are the most susceptible age groups, but it wouldn't hurt for her to have one.'

She looked across at Maddie, who was looking openly mutinous.

'I hate needles,' she said, in case Lauren hadn't got the message.

'So do I,' Lauren assured her. 'I hate getting injections and giving them, but I have to give them to keep you safe.' She turned back to Madge. 'You'll talk to Cam about the meningococcal?'

Madge nodded, then added, 'You might talk to him yourself as well, in case I don't remember.'

'Madge always forgets things,' Maddie said.

Lauren felt a twinge of alarm—older people forgetting things was something she was only too familiar with—but Madge was already speaking.

'Rubbish,' she said to the young critic. 'Although I might—just sometimes—forget to keep an eye on you when I'm fishing…'

'And one day you went home without me!' Maddie reminded her.

Poor Madge flushed. 'Not all the way home—

and that's enough, young lady. You're only talking because you think we might forget about the injection.'

Time to intercede.

'Okay, Maddie, come with me into the treatment room and we'll see just how brave you are.'

'Will I get a sweetie?' the child asked, eyeing the jar of jelly beans on Lauren's desk.

'Good children sometimes get two,' Lauren told her, with a slight emphasis on the 'good'.

In the colourful treatment room, she lifted Maddie onto an examination table and cranked it up. She was convinced, for no particular reason, that needles hurt less if you could put them straight into the muscle rather than at an angle.

Maddie was still counting some of the animals in a chart on the wall when Lauren stuck a small round plaster on the tiny hole and lowered the table.

'It's finished?' Maddie demanded. 'I didn't even feel it!'

'That's good,' Lauren told her as she lifted her to the floor.

'But will I only get one sweetie?'

Lauren smiled. 'No,' she said, 'you were especially good and can have two.'

Back in the consulting room, she opened the jar and let Maddie choose—one red and one black.

With those two clutched in her hand, she eyed the jar. 'I do like green ones too,' she said, and Lauren had to laugh.

'Nice try, kid,' she said, ruffling Maddie's hair as she propelled them out the door.

'Meningococcal—is that right?' Madge asked, and Lauren nodded.

'Just phone for an appointment any time,' she said. 'Janet will fix you up.'

But even as she ushered her next patient through the door her thoughts remained with the pair who'd just departed.

Madge and Maddie.

She *had* to think of them. Had to think of the effect any gossip might have on them—and there *would* be gossip, no matter how careful she and Cam were.

The memory of a local teenager who'd committed suicide some years earlier, unable to handle gossip about him being gay—which, as it happened, he hadn't been—was still strong in her mind. Guilt that she hadn't been able to help him still sneaked into her head when she least expected it.

Her thoughts depressed her. This whole silly thing with Cam: dinner, a few kisses, sex—very good sex—had brought light and laughter, not to mention physical pleasure, into her life, and she really didn't want to lose that.

Not just yet.

Not when simply thinking about losing it caused her pain, while thinking of *him* brought warmth flooding through her body and a bright lightness of spirit she hadn't felt for a long time.

But the idea of potentially hurtful gossip remained. Maddie was starting school soon, and Madge would begin to find interests in the area that would bring her into contact with the locals.

'So, do you think I should make an appointment to see a specialist up in Riverview?' her patient asked, and Lauren had to collect her scrambled wits and try to remember what they'd been discussing.

Stomach pain—that was it.

'A specialist would probably recommend an endoscopy—poking a tube down your throat to have a look at your stomach. But if you're only getting the pains after eating oranges, you'd be better off not eating them for a while, to see if that stops the pain completely.'

Mr March frowned at her, then lifted himself out of the chair and folded his arms across his chest. The frown turned into a full glare. 'But my tree is full of fruit,' he said. 'They're *my* oranges!'

Lauren flipped quickly through his notes— still on cards, as all the older patients' notes had yet to be computerised. And there it was. Same time every year, Mr March presented with stomach pains. Her father had actually sent him to Riverview for an endoscopy at one stage, only to be told his stomach wall lining and small intestine were all clear.

She made a new note, mentioning the oranges. She'd transfer Mr March's file to the computer this afternoon, while his visit was fresh in her mind, but in the meantime...

'Stop eating them for a few days and see how you feel,' she suggested. 'Then, if the pain disappears, try eating just one a day and see what happens.'

She made another note, and then wondered if she was overdoing the paperwork in case her mind began to slip, as her father's had—not that she'd seen the slightest sign of it in herself.

Two more patients and she was done for the morning. And, it being Thursday, she had no afternoon session. She *did* have a late volunteering shift at the sanctuary—making sure all the animals were fed and the place locked up.

Even thinking about proximity to Cam sent shivers through her body—which was stupid, given he would quite likely be out in the backblocks somewhere, tending a large animal.

She concentrated on getting a lifetime's worth of Mr March's medical history on the computer, before tidying the house. She was putting off her trip across to the sanctuary. And the decision about what to wear was definitely a little more difficult than usual…

Finally, forcing common-sense back into her head, she fixed some sandwiches for herself and the dog—he really needed a name—and headed over to the vet's place.

Henry, she decided. That would do nicely for the dog. Henry had been a fighter too—fighting for the environment, fighting against the destruction of the natural habitat—and it was far more suitable than Tramp, Scout, or any of the other names she'd considered.

'Hello, Henry,' she said to him as she entered the dim kennel.

No spoken response this time, so at least she was on her own—and, no, that *wasn't* a twinge of disappointment that ran through her body as she realised it.

She settled herself beside Henry's head, talking quietly, touching him gently, and to her surprise he responded by struggling to roll over, so he could almost sit up, one bandaged leg stuck stiffly out to the side.

'Good boy,' she said, and fed him a piece of sandwich, patting the unbandaged bits of him. 'You should be getting most of those dressings off tomorrow,' she told him, as she ate her own sandwich.

He leaned cautiously to one side, and she lifted his water bowl, certain he'd fall back down if he tried to reach it himself.

She held it to him while he drank greedily. 'So maybe, while you're up, you'd like some real food?' she said, and reached for the bowl of dried food, holding it in front of him so he could sniff at it and nuzzle a few pieces before snaffling some into his mouth with his tongue.

'Good for you!' she said, so excited she'd have given him a hug if she hadn't thought it would hurt him.

But he must have got the message, because she was sure he smiled at her—a sloppy kind of smile, but definitely recognisable.

'Oh, you darling!' she said, and gave him a little more sandwich, feeling his tongue licking at her palm.

'Haven't you heard the expression about biting the hand that feeds you?'

She turned to see Cam, stooping at the entrance to the kennel.

'He just smiled at me,' she told him, wanting to share her delight and also to cover her reaction to seeing him—equal delight!

'Oh, yes…?'

Polite disbelief, but there was a smile in his voice again, and she felt the tremor of desire fire her senses.

Damn it all! She *had* to get over this reaction to his presence—it confused her senses, stopped her thinking sensibly, and she was reasonably sure that she *had* to think sensibly about their relationship.

Cam certainly wasn't!

But the situation—gossip, her father, so many things that really should be considered... Or should have *been* considered before this went too far...

And he was married...

And the age thing...

And, on that point, wasn't she too old to be feeling such intensity of desire? Wasn't that teenage stuff? First flush of love stuff? Not that she could remember feeling tremors of desire at the mere sound of David's voice...

Deep breath. Common sense.

'When will the dressings come off, so we can see what he looks like?' she asked, determined to sound sensible and practical and not like some teenager overcome by the enormity of first love.

'I'll redo them later,' Cam said, coming to squat beside her. 'Did you come over just to have lunch with the dog?' he asked, nodding at the bundle of sandwiches she'd set on the floor.

She turned and grinned at him. 'No, I'm on duty at the sanctuary later this afternoon, so I called in to see him first. He ate a sandwich, then sat up and had water and some actual dog food. So I imagine once you unwrap him, and he has more freedom to move, he'll probably prefer that to sandwiches.'

She put her hand on the head that was now resting on her knee.

'Won't you, Henry?'

'Henry? You're going to call him Henry?'

'I think it's a great name for a noble dog like him,' she said firmly. 'I've told him our Henry was a fighter—especially for animal rights.'

Cam settled beside her, slid a hand across her shoulders and gently brushed the skin beneath her hair. Then he pressed a kiss on the back of her neck…sending shivers all over her.

She had no memory of ever reacting to a man like this, yet that single touch had relit the embers of desire that he could flame into fire so easily.

Remember Maddie and Madge and gossip! And that he's younger than you! And married!

The mantra rang in her head even as she turned towards him and let his lips meet hers.

Fat lot of good mantras did.

At least they'd both have to get back to work before anything more could happen.

The late afternoon schedule at the sanctuary was always busy, as all the animals had to be checked to see if their wounds were healing, or if some other problem might have appeared.

The wombats were the worst. Once old enough and brave enough to leave their hollow logs, they often injured their front digging paws by trying to build a burrow near a fence post that was concreted into the ground. They had to follow their instincts to dig before they could be taken back into the bush, where they'd have to dig their own protective burrows, so it was a no-win situation.

'Poor baby,' Lauren murmured to one, as she fed it the formula especially prepared for wombats.

'Poor baby nothing,' a voice growled from behind her. 'Where's my dog?'

A man—a very large man—stood outside the sanctuary fence, a shotgun dangling casually from one hand.

'I'm sorry, sir, but this is a wildlife sanctuary—we rescue wombats and koalas and such. We don't have dogs.'

She hoped she sounded a lot more confident than she felt.

'That mad woman said she brought my dog here!' the man said, moving the shotgun slightly.

'I can't let you in because the animals can pick up germs from outside, but please look around—there's only me and the animals and that store cupboard over there. You can see right into it—

nothing there. I'm sorry, but if your dog's lost maybe you could put some notices up in the village?'

'I won't put up any damn notice in the village!' the man roared. 'I'll be back!'

He turned and strode away, and now Lauren saw the ute parked in the shade of a tree some distance away. Cautiously parked, so it could barely be seen.

She remained where she was, frozen in place, until he'd driven away—not around the house to where the kennels were, but back in the direction he'd come from.

Get his number plate, some still functioning brain cell told her. But the ute was already disappearing, and all she noticed was a rusty dent in the passenger-side door.

Some clue!

She breathed deeply, realised she was holding the wee wombat far too tightly, and slowly set him down on the ground.

Police.

Aware that the one constable who was seeing out his last few years before retirement in the village wouldn't be the best person to tackle an angry man with a shotgun, she phoned the larger police station, further up the lake.

And although she'd felt tentative about phoning, wondering if it was too minor a matter to be reporting, she was greeted by reassurances that she'd done the right thing and then, to her surprise, she was transferred to someone called Brendan from 'the cattle duffing squad'.

'Cattle duffing squad?' she echoed weakly, and he laughed.

'It happens more often than you think,' Brendan assured her. 'Cattle go missing all the time, and although some have just wandered through a broken fence into a neighbour's yard, many of them are stolen, moved interstate, or sold off before they cross a border.'

'And dog-fighting?' Lauren felt compelled to ask.

'Oh, that's really nasty—and although we've been aware of a gang operating somewhere near here, we've never been able to find them. You're at the sanctuary at the end of the lake?'

Lauren agreed and the man hung up—though when exactly he or anyone else would appear she had no idea.

She'd better tell Cam he was coming, and mention the man with a gun. First, though, she would phone Helen, to let her know what was going on. Who knew what Brendan might suggest they do when he appeared. Remove all the animals?

Helen refused to panic, saying simply that

she'd get someone over there to spend the night just in case there was a disturbance.

Helen's calm rubbed off on Lauren, so phoning Cam was relatively easy—until he caught on to what had happened and reacted with protective anger, asking why she'd remained in the vicinity of a man with a gun.

After hanging up, he came straight through to the sanctuary and put his arm around her shoulders, softening any rebuke in his words.

Brendan and his mate—both in the khaki uniform of country police officers—arrived within half an hour, and assured her and Cam that the animals would be safe.

'No one will come near the sanctuary with our very obvious vehicle out there.' Brendan waved his hand towards the big khaki four-wheel drive parked just outside the fence. 'These fellows know we're just as serious as they are. In fact, more so.' He turned to Cam. 'You live in the house?' he asked, and Cam explained that he, Madge and Maddie did.

'Oh, and there's a dog and a pregnant cat out in the kennels,' Lauren added.

'Is there somewhere you can all stay for a few days? Just as a precaution?'

That was Brendan's next question, and when Cam looked totally blank, Lauren spoke up.

'They can all come to my house—it's just

over there.' She pointed in vaguely the right direction.

But she'd barely finished offering, when Cam said, 'The others can go, but I'll stay here. I won't get in your way, but I know where the tea and coffee are kept and I can provide some assistance behind the scenes.'

Brendan considered this and eventually agreed—with the proviso that Cam stayed out of their way.

'Madge and Maddie and the animals can all come to my place,' Lauren repeated. 'You were going to redress Henry's wounds. Do you want to do that first?'

Had some strain in her voice told him how anxious she was about him remaining in the house? Was that why he put his arm around her shoulders as he walked back into the surgery to get what he needed for Henry's wounds?

'I'll be fine,' he said, when he'd manoeuvred her away from the two men. He waited until he and Lauren were back in his rooms before turning to look into her face. 'I won't do anything foolish, but this *is* my house and I'll stay with it. Brendan is right—no one is likely to come with the police vehicle outside.'

'But they can't stay here for ever,' Lauren said, hoping the words didn't sound like an anguished wail.

'I don't think they'll need to. The police want to catch these people—not just chase them further underground. They'll already have a plan, so don't worry.'

He kissed her gently on the lips, then less gently as desire rose between them and passion fired the kiss.

She drew away reluctantly, aware they had things to be doing that were definitely more important than a kiss.

'I'll go and talk to Madge while you see to the dog. He can go in the mud room at my place, and the cat into the laundry. Both have doors that will shut to keep them separated.'

Cam paused only to smile at her. 'You've got it all worked out, haven't you?' he teased.

She blushed and shook her head. 'Not nearly all!' she told him, well aware that her organising was a cover for the disturbance going on inside her—a disturbance she might never work out.

'Well, it's never dull...' That was Madge's reaction to the sudden move. 'I've got dinner going in the slow cooker, so I'll just bring it along. Cam can look after himself.'

Lauren helped Madge organise Maddie's things, making sure they had Gummie and her favourite pyjamas.

Cam met them as they came down the stairs,

ready to drive them back to Lauren's place. 'Dog and pregnant cat are all packed in—now we'd better add the humans,' he said, and turned to Lauren. 'You *are* coming?' he said.

She nodded. 'There are rooms to be organised, beds to be made, and the animals to get settled.'

But I'll be back, she said to herself. She was still on duty at the sanctuary and had no intention of abandoning her post.

She climbed into Cam's four-wheel drive, next to Maddie in the back, and they set off.

Maddie was bouncing with excitement beside her. 'We're having a 'venture,' she cried to Lauren. 'Madge says there are cock—'

'Cockroaches?' Cam offered.

'Yes, them,' Maddie said. 'They're in our house and we have to sleep at your house until the spray men can get rid of them.'

'Very nasty germy things, cockroaches,' Lauren agreed, crossing her fingers surreptitiously and hoping that her guests wouldn't meet any at her house and want to move again.

It took twenty minutes to sort out bedrooms and bedlinen, bathrooms and towels. Then Maddie insisted on a quick tour of the house before finally settling herself on the floor in the laundry, talking to the cat.

'I've got to go back to see to the animals,' Lauren said quietly to Madge. 'Cam's there, and the two police officers, so I'll be quite safe. It might be a lot of fuss about nothing,' she added, 'but I feel a lot happier knowing you and Maddie are out of the house.'

'You just do what you have to do,' Madge said, patting her on the arm. 'Maddie and I will be quite fine.'

Lauren jogged back along the track as dusk was falling, arriving at Cam's house to find the police vehicle gone—although one policeman remained in the house with Cam, and Jake, another of the volunteers, was in the sanctuary.

'Helen wanted one of us here, just in case there's trouble,' he said. 'I've set up one of the sun loungers and I will probably just sleep.'

'I do hope so,' Lauren told him. 'Just remember you're here for the animals, and keep out of any trouble.'

She finished the job she'd been doing in the stock cupboard then prepared to leave—although leaving Jake there on his own didn't sit well with her.

'Go,' he said. 'I've got Cam and at least one policeman in the house, and they've set up security cameras all over the place so they can see what's happening out here. And there are back-up officers in the bush behind the place, so I'm quite safe.'

The thought of security cameras made her

decision to slip out through the side gate of the sanctuary easy, but as she took off along the path Cam appeared beside her.

'I thought you'd come in and say goodnight,' he said.

'With cameras all over the place?'

He laughed. 'They're not spying on the people inside,' he told her, slinging an arm around her shoulders and drawing her close, so she could feel the warmth of his body flow into hers. 'Anyway, I've got to get back,' he said. 'I'm fixing them something to eat. I'll walk you to the end of the path through the bush, then head home.'

And the walk home was just that. Cam escorting her—coolly and efficiently—and striding along the bush track like a guard escorting a prisoner back to prison.

Not that she wanted chat, or even kisses—which just confused her more. But this was a Cam she hadn't seen before, with tension coiled within him.

'You won't do anything stupid, will you?' she said as her house came in sight.

'The police know what they're doing,' he reminded her.

But she remembered how angry he'd been about the injuries to the dog, and knew that anger must still be burning somewhere inside him.

'We have to assume they do,' she said, and knew she sounded glum—even upset.

He smiled and bent to kiss her lips. 'I won't do anything stupid tonight,' he said, and she knew it was a promise.

But as she watched him go—striding at first, and then, when he reached the cover of the scrub, beginning to jog—she wondered if he was even capable of keeping out of trouble should it come his way...

She wanted to go back—to check on him, to stay with him in the house—but that would be stupid.

He was tired and he would want to get to bed, so he could be ready for work tomorrow, and she should do the same—after she'd settled her house guests.

Cam fed himself, and the policeman, then showed him over the place, pointing out the different exits and where doors led. After they'd cleared the kitchen table, they chose the formal dining room in the centre of the downstairs area as the best place for them to wait, as it showed no tell-tale lights to the outside.

He wasn't needed, so he left the policeman to it and returned to the kitchen, where he made sandwiches and a flask of coffee and took them through to the sanctuary. He'd met Jake earlier, and decided that the least he could do was share the man's lonely vigil.

'Food!' Jake said with delight. 'We can make tea and coffee here, but the coffee's always instant and yours smells real. And the biscuits here have all gone stale—I doubt we've tried eating them since the bushfire crisis months ago.'

'I thought I'd stay,' Cam said.

Jake smiled at him. 'I won't try to talk you out of it,' he said. 'It'll be great to have company and it means we can take shifts. I *can* make do without sleep, but I always feel it's better for my patients if I can sneak in a few hours some time during the night.'

'Doctor?'

'For my sins! I'm a paediatrician—I work up at the new children's hospital near Riverview.'

'Tough job?' Cam asked.

Jake smiled again. 'Sometimes it is, but at other times I can't think of anything more rewarding—and those are the times you have to remember, rather than dwelling on the bad ones.'

They chatted amiably for a while, eating the sandwiches and drinking the coffee. Cam opted for the first shift, and Jake settled on one of the sun loungers.

As the night wore on, with no visitors, Cam wondered if it was all for nothing—which should have made him relieved, not cranky about the whole thing.

He found another folded sun lounger and sat for a while.

Within minutes, it seemed, he was awoken by Lauren.

'Well, you two proved terrific night watchmen,' she said. 'I'd guess you had no visitors!'

Aware he must be looking sheepish, he turned to Jake, who seemed far too fresh for someone who'd slept on the uncomfortable lounger.

'Sorry, Lauren,' Jake said. 'It was probably my shift. I'll just have a quick wash and be off.'

Lauren smiled at him. 'Have a quick wash, certainly, but then come into the house. Madge tells me there's plenty of bacon and a dozen eggs in the fridge. I'll cook you both some breakfast and make coffee.'

'Will you be all right here, or do you want to use a bathroom in the house?' Cam asked Jake, who shook his head and headed for the meagre washroom facilities behind the store room.

'You go right ahead,' he said. 'And please tell Lauren thanks, but I won't stay for breakfast. I want to see my wife and kids before I go to work.'

His words—*'I want to see my wife and kids'*—stayed with Cam as he headed inside, calling to

Lauren in the kitchen before hurrying upstairs to shower and change.

He'd enjoyed being married, and had probably taken it for granted that his wife had as well. But these last two years or so, when he'd been on his own, he'd become aware that his life was incomplete in some way. Not that he'd ever given it much serious thought—he'd just got on with things. Yet what he felt now was envy, he supposed, for Jake, having a wife and kids waiting at home for him.

As he hurriedly showered and dressed the thoughts continued to chase through his head, bringing the realisation that it was Jake's emotion—his wanting to see his family—that he envied.

Because that wanting spoke of love.

'You look good for a man who spent the night on what must be the world's most uncomfortable bed,' Lauren said as Cam walked into the kitchen. 'I'm just going to slam your breakfast down on the table and hurry back—I start work in twenty minutes and I need to check my patient list.'

She set down his plate on the already set table. There was toast in the rack, the coffee pot tantalising his senses, but as she turned away he caught her hand and drew her back.

'Let's get married,' he said, pulling her down so he could kiss her lips.

She responded to the kiss, but quickly pulled away.

'*You,*' she said severely. 'For all you look okay, you're clearly suffering from a lack of proper sleep. And what is it with you and the marriage thing? A lot of men see it more as a life sentence rather than something to rush into—and yet, although you happen to already be married, you continue to suggest it to me.'

He thought for a minute, not wanting to admit that it had been Jake's words that had brought marriage back into focus in his mind.

'I liked being married,' he said. 'The being married part more so than the marriage itself, if I'm honest. To me it was always one of those things—you grow up, get married, get a job and a house, and that's how the future is mapped out. It was what I always wanted—to grow up and get married.'

'It might be a child's dream for the future,' Lauren said, although she *was* smiling as she said it, 'but so's being a princess or a superhero.'

He shrugged, because somehow he couldn't explain it better. Unless…

'Jake didn't wait for breakfast because he wanted to go home and see his wife and kids before he went to work,' he told her. 'It's that part of being married I want.'

'Or think you want,' Lauren said gently.

Cam had sounded so gloomy that Lauren was tempted to stay, but she'd already had two late starts and she didn't want to risk Janet's disapproval with another.

'I've patients to see. We'll talk later,' she said, and whisked out through the door before she weakened.

'At least you've *got* patients,' he muttered.

As she hurried home she thought about what he'd said—not the getting married part, for all that it gave her a secret longing every time he mentioned it, but about patients. Not hers, but his.

He needed to be busy and for some reason the veterinary practice *wasn't* busy.

Henry's practice had always been a busy one, and she'd assumed it would remain the same, but now she thought about it she'd seen fewer cars there lately, and she knew Cam had had fewer call-outs because he'd been around so much.

Damn.

The locum must have let it run down—or maybe been so impossible that people had simply stopped coming.

CHAPTER EIGHT

LAUREN WASN'T THE only one worrying about client numbers at the vets.

Cam finished his breakfast and walked back into his rooms to find a total stranger sitting behind his reception desk. Pretty in a *young* way—that was the only way he could describe the girl with dark curls and a bright smile.

'Hi, I'm Debbie, and I'm your new nurse—from the agency, you know? I know I wasn't supposed to start until Monday, but I wasn't doing anything today and Harry—he's my boyfriend—was coming over here on a job, so I came along to get a feel for the place.' She paused for a moment, before adding, 'That's okay, isn't it?'

He must have nodded, because she was off again.

'I've been looking through your appointment book and it's terrible, isn't it?'

He hoped it was tiredness that made him want to strangle her. It was not that someone so bright and chatty wouldn't be good for business. It was just that he couldn't handle bright and chatty this morning.

He headed straight into his surgery—hiding—but he was aware she was quite right. His appointment book did look terrible.

The return of Brendan, one of the policemen from the day before, provided relief. 'You don't seem busy, so come and see what we've discovered,' he said.

After telling Debbie to call him if he was needed, Cam followed Brendan into the house.

'I'll just have a look around, so I'll know where things are,' Debbie said, as if she needed to justify her position.

'The man did return—with mates,' Brendan told him, leading him to one of the laptops open on the dining room table.

'So much for the two guardians of the sanctuary,' Cam muttered.

Brendan laughed. 'They came quietly this time, and they had obviously heard about the kennels because they searched there first. We had men ready to go if they approached the sanctuary, but they didn't go near it or the house—no doubt assuming we'd left men inside, even though our vehicle was gone.'

'So they got away?' Cam said, anger stirring again at the treatment of the dog.

'Not cleanly,' Brendan assured him. 'We had a drone follow them to what we're assuming is their headquarters and a possible dog-fight site near an abandoned farm out towards the mountains. As soon as we get a chance we'll send someone in to check the place out. And we're using drones to keep an eye on things there in the meantime.'

'Sounds great,' Cam agreed. He was still anxious to see the men involved caught and punished, but when he thought about it he was also pleased to have professionals in charge.

And now that he had Debbie, who would alert him should a patient arrive, he could stay on with the policemen, checking the screens that showed the different shots the drones had taken as they followed the route towards the mountains.

But the men were packing up now, telling him they'd keep in touch, and he tossed up whether to go back into his rooms and face Debbie, or make himself coffee and a sandwich and have a think about patient numbers.

The coffee won.

'Anyone home?'

Madge and Maddie had gone into the village, so Lauren had finished her shift and come across to Cam's to find out what was happening, but the place seemed deserted.

She'd tried the surgery rooms first, and seen a note from someone named Debbie saying she'd gone to lunch, and the sanctuary had yielded only Helen, so now she stood in the big entry, calling out for Cam.

'Kitchen!' Cam answered, and she headed there to find him sitting at the kitchen table, a pen in his hand and a writing pad on the table in front of him.

'I've been thinking about your lack of patients,' she said, 'and I've had some ideas.'

He looked up at her and grinned. 'Me too, but I'll need help to know what will work.'

'I was thinking the local paper first,' Lauren said. 'The *Lake News*—Madge might have brought home a copy. It's printed right here in the village, but it goes around the lake. You could do an "Ask the Vet" column once a week.'

Cam's grin made her heart flip just a little, and his fingers tangled with hers as he passed her his list.

'Third idea down,' he said. 'Now, come and sit beside me and we'll go through them. You want coffee?'

'Yes, please—and a sandwich if you can manage one. I came straight from work and I really want to hear what's happening with the police.'

'You go through the list while I fix you something, then we can talk.' There was a slight pause before he tease, 'If that's what you *really* want to do?'

She frowned at him. 'Yes, it is. This is serious! I want to know about the dog-fights...but, far more important, you can't just let Henry's business die—'

She stopped, looking at him, searching his face, wondering...

'Unless that's what you want?' she whispered, with thoughts of him selling the house and fleeing back to England to domestic pets and no possibility of a snake in his house swirling through her mind.

He crossed to the table and put an arm around her shoulders, giving her a gentle hug. 'Don't be silly,' he said. 'Take a look at my list and then tell me if I'm thinking of abandoning Henry's gift to me.'

The arm around her shoulders was reassuring—as was the list, now she looked at it. But the gut-wrenching, heart-stopping pain she'd felt when—just for a moment—she'd imagined him gone, told her how completely she was entangled with him now...how deep her emotions ran and how very important he'd become to her.

And yet she knew she was all wrong for him. She concentrated on his list and actually smiled, because every single thing she'd thought of was there.

'Henry had a weekly talk on local radio,' she said to Cam, who'd returned to his coffee and sandwich-making. 'Just ten minutes, and he covered things like the best way to treat midge bites as well as animal health.'

Cam put coffee and a plate of sandwiches in front of her, then pulled out a chair so they sat together, thighs touching, the heat of his body transferring to hers.

'And how *do* you treat a midge bite?'

Lauren grinned at him. 'I'm not sure I remember Henry's advice because they never worry me. I think I've grown immune to them. But when in doubt use vinegar, my father always said. For bluebottle stings in the sea in summer, midge and sand fly bites—vinegar or bicarb soda: his panaceas for most painful bites and stings.'

'Apart from funnel web spiders?'

Lauren had to laugh. 'Definitely not spiders of any kind! Spider bites you need to treat like a snake bite. You should keep four or five elasticised bandages somewhere handy, then you can bandage over the bite, down to the extremity of the arm or leg then back up again, phoning an ambulance as you do it.'

'Really?' Cam asked.

She nodded, because even a sensible conversation about health matters hadn't quelled the disturbances caused by Cam's proximity, and she was reasonably sure there'd be a tremor in her voice if she tried to speak.

She moved her chair, just a little, and pulled the notepad towards her, and together they went through their ideas to give his animal patient numbers a boost.

'I really should be going,' she said suddenly.

'You've only just arrived,' he said, taking her hand in his, folding her fingers so it fitted inside his palm.

It was hand-holding, nothing more—yet for some reason it was so erotic she squirmed in her seat.

She removed her hand from his clasp and shifted her chair a little further away.

'We're going to drink coffee, eat our lunch and talk about your list,' she said firmly.

'Even though we're all alone in this great big house?' he murmured, and the rasp of his voice scratched at her skin.

'I'm back!'

The call came just in time, and while Cam went to welcome his new employee properly Lauren hastily ate a sandwich and drained her coffee, then departed, yelling goodbye through the surgery door.

Madge and Maddie would be back from the village and wanting to get in, she told herself as she hurried away.

But she knew she was hurrying *from*—not hurrying *to*.

She forced herself to slow down, finding an even pace that would allow her to think.

But how to think about Cam?

About the way he made her feel?

About the physical reactions he could cause in her body with nothing more than a glance?

And why him?

She *had* met other men over the years since David, but none had turned both her mind and her body into such a state of turmoil.

She paused, forcing herself to think, telling herself she was a mature middle-aged woman and she should be able to rationalise this...whatever it was...

But standing still didn't help—and it didn't stop her hearing Cam's teasing voice in her ears, or feeling his touch on her skin...

'You've been called out to the alpaca farm.'

Cam was startled by the voice as he made his way back into the surgery. Once again, he'd forgotten he had a new nurse. He really would have to sit down and have a talk with her—find out about her qualifications, things like that—

but for now just having someone to answer the phone was a bonus.

'Thank you,' he said. 'I hope it won't take long and we can have a chat when I get back. In the meantime...'

He pulled his list out of his pocket and found Lauren had put ticks against some of his ideas— two or three ticks in some cases.

'Do you think putting leaflets into letter-boxes around the lake, telling people I'm here, is a good idea?' he asked Debbie.

'An excellent one,' she said. 'I was doodling something on the computer that might do.'

She swung the screen to show a page with cats, dogs, birds and, yes, alpacas, depicted around the edge, with his name, address and phone number clearly printed in the middle. Then he noticed the heading:

Under new management!
Henry's nephew has arrived!

'That looks great,' he said, 'but is it okay to put the bit about Henry?'

She smiled at him. 'Everyone loved Henry,' she said, as if that automatically meant they'd all love Cam too.

But he knew full well he'd have to prove him-self—and it appeared he'd have a lot to live up to.

Debbie was speaking again. 'You'd better get out to the alpacas—something about pregnancy testing? That Celia out there does run on and on.'

Pots and kettles, Cam thought, leaving Debbie to her work and getting the portable ultrasound out of the equipment cupboard.

Debbie was printing off the leaflets when he came back through the reception area.

'I'll stay on and answer the phone and print out more leaflets—do some larger ones for shop windows,' she said. 'Your mother phoned to say she'll be back soon, so I won't leave to put up the posters until after she comes. Is that okay?'

Still befuddled by the force that was Debbie, Cam nodded, locked the treatment room door, and departed.

Lauren, taking advantage of finishing early, had decided to walk Maddie and Madge back to their home. The dog and the cat would stay at her place, and she'd bring their gear over later.

'There's Daddy going out!' cried Maddie, who was running on ahead, and they saw the four-wheel drive reversing out of the garage.

'Stop where you are,' Madge called to Maddie, who obeyed immediately, although she was bouncing up and down with excitement at seeing her father.

Cam stopped and climbed out, swinging his

daughter into the air and settling her on his hip, giving Lauren a twinge of something she couldn't understand. Not jealousy, certainly, but perhaps a kind of envy at the picture they made.

The *family* they made.

'Are you done for the morning?' Cam asked.

Lauren nodded. 'We have a very healthy population around here.'

'Same with animals,' he said. 'But if you're free, I could do with a hand.'

'Can I come too, Daddy?' Maddie asked.

Cam shook his head. 'Not today, sweetie— but go on in and say hello to my new vet nurse, Debbie.'

Maddie skipped away to catch up with Madge.

'Debbie?' Lauren asked as she climbed in the car, her pleasure at seeing Cam only slightly marred by the warnings of that stupid voice in her head—that useless mantra…

'Believe me, you can't possibly be as surprised as I was when she turned up and—'

'And started talking—if she's Debbie Bradley from further up the lake?'

'That's the one,' Cam said.

Lauren laughed. 'She's actually very good, and people trust her. I'm sure she'll give the practice the boost it needs.'

'It's almost as if she's read my list…'

He turned to look at Lauren, sharing his rueful despair, and she saw the gleam of amusement in his blue eyes and felt her heart contract.

She loved him.

It wasn't so much a question as a certainty that had suddenly struck right at her heart.

Just like that, out of nowhere, the realisation had come—and she had no idea what to do with it or about it.

She was too old for him—she knew that... knew he needed a younger woman. Someone who'd get him involved in the social life of the area—such as it was—who would have parties and go to music festivals...all the things young people in their twenties did.

She also knew she couldn't condemn him to what might lie ahead.

The shadow of her father's illness sat like a black cloud above her head whenever Cam's silly idea of marriage was mentioned. Dementia wasn't necessarily a genetic disease, but it did have genetic links in some families. Her father had often spoken of his 'mad grandmother', who, Lauren suspected, had probably had it too.

And, knowing the soul-destroying task that caring for a loved one with dementia could be, how could she risk handing that on to Cam—ten years younger than she was, who would probably still be a very active man at fifty-five if she, like her father, had her first symptoms at sixty-five?

'Anything that can help build the practice,' she said, realising it was her turn to speak in their conversation, and thankfully remembering where it had stopped.

But her mind wasn't on it. It was far too busy coping with what was in her heart.

Damn it all—why couldn't life be easy?

Hadn't she been happy enough before this man had erupted into her life?

Satisfied with her lot?

Enjoying her life?

She was happy to have an affair with him—delighted, in fact—but marriage…?

'So I think Celia will run them through the chute she has out there, and isolate one animal at a time, so all we'll have to do is the ultrasound. I'm reasonably sure she can read the screen as well as I can, but having you there to hold it will be a blessing.'

And Lauren was a blessing in other ways, Cam thought, remembering Jake's eagerness to see his wife and kids, and feeling aware of how good it was simply to have her by his side.

And a lot later in that day he'd be aware that he'd never have managed without her…

As they drove up—not towards the house, but to the paddock near the chute, where they could see Celia waiting—the woman suddenly fell to the grass.

Cam pulled up as close as he safely could, and he and Lauren both shot out and raced towards the fallen woman.

'Celia? Celia, can you hear me?' Lauren shouted as she ran, then she dropped to her knees and gave the woman a little shake, feeling at the same time for a pulse beneath her neck.

Cam reached Celia's side just as Lauren checked her mouth, then gave her two full breaths of air.

'Ring triple zero,' she said to Cam as she began compressions, counting aloud as she went.

He made the call, then dropped to his knees. 'I'll take over here—you do the breaths,' he said.

Lauren reached thirty and sank back, again feeling for a pulse.

'Nothing?' Cam asked, and Lauren shook her head.

'There might be,' she said, 'but if there is it's very weak. Often it's hard to tell, so we'll just keep going.'

He had kept the compressions going, and again Lauren breathed air into Celia's unconscious body. But this time, as Cam continued compressions, she ran her hands over Celia's head, feeling for any contusions.

There were no trees with branches she could

have hit—in fact there was nothing at all anywhere near her that could have knocked her out.

'I'll do these breaths, then we'll swap,' she
said to Cam, aware how tiring compressions
could be, even on practice dummies.

'I'm fine.'

It was the response she'd expected. 'Yes, for
now you are. But if we have to wait thirty minutes for an ambulance, you won't be.'

The look of disbelief he gave her was price-
less, but he didn't argue when she took over once
he'd reached thirty. Lauren counted while she
watched him administer air, then looked around
in frustration. She imagined the city streets
where he'd lived regularly rang with the sirens
of approaching fire engines or ambulances.

'It won't be too much longer,' she said, and
as if conjured up by her voice an ambulance appeared, the big four-wheel drive vehicle coming
smoothly across the paddock towards them.

Cam explained that they'd actually seen Celia
fall and phoned immediately, while the paramedic fitted an oxygen mask to Celia's mouth
and nose, then attached a valve bag to it to deliver continuous positive pressure air.

'Can you hold your thumbs to the mask either side of her mouth to seal it?' the paramedic
asked Cam.

Lauren got out of the way as the second paramedic knelt by Celia's side with a resuscitator, fixing pads to her skin, checking lines and preparing to shock her heart.

The 'Clear!' signal rang out and they all moved slightly back.

The paramedic closest to Cam felt for a pulse once she'd been shocked. He shook his head, then held up a hand. 'Maybe...' he said. 'It's faint and thready, but it's there, I'm sure.'

They shocked her heart a second time, with a steadier result.

'Okay, we'll take it from here,' one of the paramedics said, and in what seemed like a remarkably short time they had her loaded into the ambulance and were driving away.

'Poor Celia,' Cam said.

'Poor you,' Lauren replied with a grin.

'Me? What? Why me?'

Lauren's smile broadened. 'Well, as well as having to preg-test the alpacas without her help, you're now going to have to work out how to look after them while Celia's off in hospital.'

'Me?'

'You're the vet,' she reminded him. 'Now, let's get on with what we came to do, and later we'll think about the animals.'

Cam, still shaken by seeing Celia so stricken, decided that was a very good suggestion—

although it was slowly dawning on him that he couldn't just abandon the animals. There was plenty of grass in the paddock, but they would need some supplementary feeding, water, and definite overseeing.

Should he forget the pregnancy testing and just seek out someone to keep an eye on them? Then visit Celia in hospital and tell her he'd not done the job?

He didn't think so.

'Okay, let's go,' he said, retrieving his gear from the car, passing the laptop to Lauren and grabbing the bag with the ultrasound machine, thrusting away the thought that perhaps they could have used it on Celia, to see if her heart had been beating.

Stupid! It would have wasted precious time.

Alpacas—that was where his head had to be.

The animals had already been herded into a small paddock close to the chute, but the beasts weren't the silly, friendly creatures they'd appeared to be on first acquaintance. They circled towards the chute and then ducked off at the last minute, with Lauren herding them, while he stood ready to push the sliding gate across to secure them one at a time for the test.

'They must be friends,' Lauren said—totally unhelpfully—as two of the alpacas tried to cram into the chute together. 'Where one goes, the other goes.'

She was trying to use a garden rake she'd picked up to hold one of them back, but didn't have a hope.

Cam tried pushing the other one backwards, but got nowhere.

'Can you possibly do them both while they're crammed in like that?' Lauren asked. 'Maybe you do the one on your side, then we'll swap gear and I'll do the one on this side.'

Cam shook his head at just how much his professional life had changed, but as they successfully tested both animals with just a little extra effort—clambering up onto the lowest rung of the chute to swap implements—he found himself enjoying it all.

'Did you put the ear tag number of the one you tested onto the computer?' Lauren asked.

He looked blankly at her. 'Damn and blast!' he said. 'I didn't give it a thought—didn't even think about recording things at all...just the actual testing. But of course it has to be recorded.'

'No worries. We've got all the numbers, and if those two stay together we'll find her later.'

'It *might* be possible,' Cam answered through gritted teeth, as the next so-called pet bit his shoulder.

Somehow they got through all the animals, finding only three not pregnant. They also discovered that Celia had adjusted the gates so the animals left the chute and went into a fresh, grassy paddock with a feeding trough along one side. All the animals had headed towards it, which made it easier for them to find the pair that had refused to be separated.

Their ear tags, when checked, were forty-one and forty-two, suggesting they might be twins.

Finally, the paperwork was complete.

'And now all we have to do is find someone to keep an eye on them,' Cam said.

But Lauren was already heading for the house.

'Celia has a married daughter who lives in the area,' she said as he caught up with her. 'We'll find a phone number somewhere. And we'll have to lock up the house. We don't get much theft around here, but there are always opportunistic people who might hear she's been hospitalised and come for a look around.'

She was right, he realised, and relief that she'd agreed to come with him flooded through him. As things had turned out, he certainly couldn't have managed without her. But her presence, he thought as he followed her towards the house, was unsettling him rather than bringing the usual joy.

It was Jake's fault, of course—though he wasn't to know that a casual remark about wanting to see his wife and kids would ruin Cam's day.

Ruin his day?

What on earth was he thinking?

'Self-pity never gets you anywhere,' he could hear his mother's voice telling him.

But, hell...

He was a grown man with a daughter—what he was feeling surely couldn't be self-pity.

It was nothing more than irritation with the bloody alpacas, for whom he had yet to develop any fondness.

Shaking off his wayward thoughts, because there was work still to be done, he followed Lauren into the house, catching her in the kitchen and giving her a hug.

She turned to face him, a *What was that for?* question in her eyes, but somehow their lips met and the hug became a kiss.

And, given the way he'd been feeling all morning, it was only with the strongest of will power that he refrained from mentioning the marriage thing again.

Refrained from just asking on the off-chance...

Because he couldn't get it out of his head...

* * *

'Enough!' Lauren said, breaking away and pointing him towards the list held by a magnet to the door of the refrigerator. 'Ellen—that's her daughter,' she said, her finger on a name. 'I'll phone her, because she knows me, and she'll be able to tell us who to call to keep an eye on the animals. Would you mind going through the house and closing the windows, locking the outside doors, and—'

'Checking there are no appliances left on?' he finished for her.

She grinned at him. 'Okay, I know you know as well as I do how to check things out. It's just me being—'

'Bossy?'

'Go!' she ordered. 'I've got a difficult call to make.'

It took another half-hour to make sure the family knew what had happened, to check on Celia's status at the hospital—she was in Intensive Care—and to organise a neighbour to take care of the alpacas.

They were fairly quiet on the drive back. Lauren was still testing the revelation that had struck her earlier about her feelings for this man. She found herself sneaking quick glances at him, as if seeing him in profile, or talking, or frowning over something, might help her work out why she was feeling as she did—why she'd been stupid enough to actually fall in love with him.

He was just a man, after all.

A nice man—well, mostly. He was crabby when he was in pain, but who wasn't?

And it wasn't as if she hadn't met other nice men over the years—even gone out with several of them while Henry sat with her father. But the truly weird, heart-clenching realisation of love had never featured in any of those brief relationships.

Maybe it wasn't love she felt for Cam. Maybe it was just some kind of heart arrhythmia and he'd just happened to be there when it happened…

Several times.

Almost constantly, actually.

She sighed, even though she'd thought she'd given up sighing.

'You okay?' he asked.

She nodded. Then, because his eyes were on the road, she added, 'Fine.'

Time to take control, she decided. *Forget this heart-love business!*

'Have you heard anything from Brendan?' she asked, but he shook his head.

'He doubted anything would happen before the weekend, and he's got the place he thinks is their headquarters covered by drones.'

Back at the surgery, they found a note from Debbie explaining that she and a friend were dropping notices in letterboxes and there'd been no phone calls.

But the note didn't finish there.

We've taken Maddie with us, so we won't go far.

Madge said it would be okay, but here's my mobile number if you want to check.

Debbie had then listed her number, and her boyfriend Harry's number for any emergency, and signed off with a flourish, a little heart dotting the 'i' in her name.

'Even in a note she talks a lot,' Cam said gloomily.

Lauren laughed at him. 'Go on with you,' she said. 'Debbie is just what you need to brighten this place up.' She looked around and added, 'Well, a coat of paint wouldn't go amiss either!'

But their conversation, although relieving Lauren's fears about the dog-fighting man returning, had done little to dispel the aftershocks of the discovery she'd had made on the drive to the alpaca farm. The certainty of this love thing had left her mind and her body churning helplessly.

It could go nowhere—she knew that—even if the wretched man mentioned marriage at least once a day.

It just felt wrong. And the age difference, her fear of potentially facing dementia herself one day, and the suddenness made it all the more overwhelming.

CHAPTER NINE

SHE'D BARELY OPENED her afternoon session when Cam arrived, with a drowsy, unresponsive Maddie in his arms.

'Call an ambulance,' she said to Janet, as soon as she saw the child.

She ushered Cam inside her office.

'What happened?' she asked as she checked Maddie's temperature—thirty-nine degrees—something the flushed face and body had already suggested.

'She went to her bedroom to have a rest and then we couldn't wake her,' Cam said, his voice coarse with panic and concern.

She injected paracetamol into the child's limp arm and brought damp cloths to bathe the burning skin.

Meningococcal had been Lauren's first thought, and shame that she'd let events at the sanctuary take precedence over talking to Cam about the vaccination gnawed at her stomach. But as she checked Maddie's body she saw there were no tell-tale signs of the disease. She was flushed all over, but with no darker spots or splotches.

'She'll be safe in the ambulance and you can travel with her,' she said to Cam, hoping her voice would be enough to calm him down a little. 'I'll come up later, bring Madge and clothes. There's a new children's hospital just south of Riverview—it's about three-quarters of an hour's drive. There's accommodation attached to it where you and Madge can stay. I'll arrange all that when I get there.'

She wasn't sure he'd heard any of it. His whole being was focussed on willing his child to keep breathing.

The ambulance arrived, and with the paramedics' usual seamless efficiency sped away within minutes.

Lauren saw them off, then phoned Madge.

Of course Madge wanted to go, so Lauren explained that she'd collect her at six and reminded her to pack a few things for Cam, as well as for herself and Maddie.

'And some story books and a toy or two,' she added, then hung up to get back to her patients.

By the time Lauren and Madge arrived at the hospital that evening Maddie had been admitted to the ICU.

Cam kissed them both, but looked so utterly weary that Lauren handed him a bag of clothes and toiletries and sent him across to the accommodation block to have a shower and a rest.

'You're booked in there. Madge and I will both stay with Maddie while you take a break,' Lauren told him.

'Jake's here—from the sanctuary. He said he'd look after her. He did a lumbar puncture,' Cam said, in a helpless voice that made her want to hug him. 'But I don't think the results are back yet. He's thinking meningitis.'

'They'll all look after her—and we'll be with her. You go and rest.'

He kissed her again, and left reluctantly.

'Isn't that what we were talking about when I brought her in to see you?' Madge asked.

Lauren shook her head. 'Meningococcal is slightly different,' she told her. 'If this is a viral infection, rather than a bacterial one, I doubt a vaccination would have made a difference. A viral infection is most likely to have come from a virus Maddie's picked up somewhere. It could have been something as small as someone sneezing in a shop.'

'We were in town the other day and every second person seemed to have a cold,' Madge said. 'And she's been playing in that old shed a lot lately.'

Lauren shook her head. She knew you could eat off the floor of Henry's shed. Even as he'd grown older, his long-time cleaning woman would come and clean it weekly.

'She *has* been a bit sniffly lately,' Madge said, the vague tone suggesting that she was running back through Maddie's life over the last few weeks.

'Stop fretting about it,' Lauren said firmly. 'Whatever has happened has happened, and now Maddie needs us. Which is her favourite book? I'll read it to her.'

To Lauren's surprise, Madge handed her a very old copy of *Winnie the Pooh*, which Lauren recognised as one that had belonged to Henry as a child. She'd borrowed it to read herself, many times.

She smoothed her hand over the rather tired blue cover, then opened it and began to read.

Maddie's condition barely changed over the next two days—the little girl remained either asleep or too drowsy to do anything other than smile weakly at whoever had appeared at her bedside.

So when Lauren came to relieve Cam at midnight three days later, sitting next to him and holding his hand, she broached a subject she wasn't at all sure he'd want mentioned.

'Do you think her mother should be told?'

she asked. 'You said she was in Australia at the moment.'

He frowned at her, shook his head, then nodded.

'I have let her know,' he said. 'I phoned her the night Maddie was admitted. She *is* in Australia—up north somewhere in the rainforest. She sends a card to Maddie from time to time. Usually with a lizard on it—Aboriginal paintings of lizards. Snakes too.'

'And…?' Lauren prompted.

Cam shook his head as if trying to focus. 'I think she said she'd come, but that she had things to arrange. She has my number, so I suppose she'll let me know.'

It all seemed very vague and totally unsatisfactory to Lauren, but she knew it was none of her business, and she didn't want to push Cam in the state he was already in.

But Maddie's mother—Kate—*did* arrive. On Sunday afternoon she swept into the hospital in a blaze, scattering 'darlings' at all the staff, crying by her daughter's bedside, then pronouncing herself utterly spent and asking to be shown to her room.

She took the room Lauren had been using. Lauren had packed and left that morning, explaining to Madge that she'd be more use back at the lake, organising Cam's practice and getting back to her own work.

Kate was still Cam's wife and the mother of Maddie. A *good* mother, she remembered Cam saying. Lauren knew she was best off out of the way.

But if Lauren's departure from the scene was low key, Kate's arrival had been anything but. The local newspaper, always eager for a bit of glamour to lift its otherwise provincial status, had caught a shot of her arrival at the airport. And the front page that greeted Lauren when she picked up the paper from her doorstep on Monday morning was highlighted by a photograph of a beautiful, petite blonde woman, a filmy handkerchief clutched in one hand.

Above it, in what seemed to Lauren to be an unnecessarily large font, were the words *UK Actress Arrives to Sit by Ill Daughter!*

Actress?

How come that had never been mentioned? she thought.

Or maybe it had…

A beautiful blonde actress…

It was even worse than Lauren had thought.

They'd married while at university, Madge had said—in rather disapproving tones. But maybe only Cam had been at university—

unless Kate had been doing a drama degree of some kind?

And Cam had enjoyed being married.

That he *had* told Lauren.

Cam had phoned Maddie's mother, assuming she'd be too busy, or too involved with whatever she was involved in, to want to come.

So her, 'I'll be there as soon as I can,' had come as something of a surprise.

Until he picked up a paper in one of the hospital waiting rooms and saw the photo and the headline. As far as he knew, journalists didn't stalk the small, regional airport in anticipation of celebrities arriving—and even if they did, they'd have seen a pretty woman but would not have had any idea of her name.

Unless she'd organised the reception committee herself. Which meant, he decided, after tossing around several alternatives, that she was probably looking for work in Australia and needed a bit of free publicity.

The thought made his heart sink.

Madge had lived with them since Maddie's birth—Kate having assured him that children who grew up in multi-generation households were more stable—and even though she'd only come to help out with the new baby, she had soon become the main caregiver—and indispensable in that role, given that Kate was rarely home.

It had been Madge that Maddie had always turned to—either in excitement or concern—and Kate's departure had barely caused a blip in Maddie's existence.

But maybe he was wrong to be cynical about Kate's arrival now. She might have found some deeply buried maternal instinct and need to be with her child.

He wasn't entirely taken in by the tears she'd shed at Maddie's bedside. And yet she had sat there for nearly an hour, reading a book she'd brought about animals in the rainforest and generally becoming the centre of attention in the ward—far more than the usual number of doctors and nurses had just 'popped in' to see how Maddie was doing.

'Like hell!' Cam muttered through gritted teeth, as he thought of Kate playing the doting mother to his sleeping child.

Where was Lauren when he needed her? He needed her common-sense and calm, supportive comfort. Needed her presence by his side and, yes, her body in his bed, so he could lose his fear and dread, even for a brief time, as he lost himself inside her.

Had he conjured her up? Because she appeared

early that evening, offering to sit with Maddie so he could spend some time with his wife.

She was as lovely as ever, and her smile warmed his blood, but Kate was dragging him away, informing him that he should take her somewhere special for dinner as she'd come all this way to see them both.

And when Lauren raised her eyebrows in a quizzical manner at this statement, he hoped Kate didn't notice...

She *was* gorgeous, Cam's wife, Lauren conceded to herself as the pair departed. Big blue eyes, a neat nose and full red lips—all set in pale, creamy skin, the lot framed by short, almost white-blonde pixie-cut hair.

It would be good for Maddie if they got back together—wouldn't it?

Two parents were better than one, weren't they?

She really didn't know. She'd grown up with just a father and she was okay.

Wasn't she?

Forget it.

She set aside a book about animals in a jungle—or was it a rainforest?—which looked far too complex for a four-year-old, and returned to reading about Pooh and his friends, getting a slight response when Maddie opened her eyes and said, 'Lauren…?'

'I'm here, sweetheart,' Lauren told her, gently squeezing the fingers of one small hand. 'And I'll stay right here with you until Daddy gets back, okay?'

'And Puss?'

The words were slurred, but Lauren knew what she was asking. 'No kittens yet, but it can't be long. I'll tell you as soon as something happens.'

As Maddie sighed, then slipped back into a deep sleep, Lauren wiped silly tears from her face and began to read again. She'd brought along her own copy of *The House at Pooh Corner* for after she'd finished this one, and was actually loving reading about Pooh's life again…

She was singing nursery songs from her childhood, very softly, when Cam returned—without his beautiful wife—close to eleven that evening.

'Are you going to drive back home when you leave here?' he demanded.

She smiled, and took his hand, pulled him down into the chair beside her. 'Sit, relax,' she ordered, then put her arm around his shoulders and drew him closer in an awkward hug.

As she released him, she took both his hands in hers, and looked deep into his haunted eyes.

'She's going to be okay,' she said firmly. 'She roused earlier and spoke to me—knew me—and she asked about the cat. It's a great sign, Cam. She just needs time and plenty of rest.'

And because his smile was so pathetic, and she sensed that he, too, was fighting tears, she kept talking.

'Anyway, I wanted to tell you about what's happening back in the other world. That Debbie certainly is a whirlwind. She got on to a vet she used to work for—he's retired now, and lives on the lake—and she has him coming in to cover for you. And she's put leaflets in letterboxes and posters in shop windows, and she says if she stays as busy as she is now you'll need a receptionist as well as her on your staff.'

Cam shook his head. 'I hardly know the girl—woman, I suppose—and she's doing all this for me.'

Lauren laughed. 'People are basically good, you know. By now everyone will have heard that Maddie's sick, and one thing the Lakes community does well is rally around. There are probably enough casseroles in your freezer to keep you all fed for a month!'

He smiled, and Lauren knew he'd finally relaxed.

'Go and get some sleep. I'm happy to stay tonight and doze here—it's an ability doctors have, to be able to sleep anywhere at any time. I'll go home in time for work in the morning and I can sleep in my afternoon break.'

He shook his head. 'I can't have you doing that,' he said.

She smiled at him. 'I know—but I also know that if you don't get a proper night's sleep you'll be no good to anyone tomorrow, and by tomorrow Maddie might be well enough to talk to you, or at least smile.' She paused, and when he said nothing, she added, 'Go!' in her most authoritative voice and pointed to the door.

He leant across the space between them and kissed her on the lips. Then he stood up, kissed Maddie on the forehead, and left the room.

He did sleep, deeply and dreamlessly, waking with a start at four in the morning.

Refreshed, he showered and shaved, then dressed in his last set of clean clothes—he'd have to find a laundromat somewhere or make a trip home today. He made himself a coffee, and ate a day-old sandwich out of the refrigerator, then headed across to the hospital.

He stopped at the ICU desk, to hear the latest on his daughter's progress, and was told she'd actually asked for water during the night and let Lauren give it to her from a glass. So his step was lighter as he made his way to Maddie's room—and probably lightened more by the thought of seeing Lauren.

He found her where he'd left her, sitting in the same chair, reading quietly to his sleeping daughter.

He looked at the pair of them and knew that this was what he really wanted in his life—these two, dear, precious people.

'Did you sleep?' the one who was awake asked him, and he nodded, his throat so tight with emotion he couldn't express it in words.

Instead, he crossed the room and kissed her, then drew her to her feet and held her, snug in his arms, while he looked at Maddie and smiled.

'I've got to go,' the precious woman in his arms was saying, edging away from him. 'Did the nurse tell you she woke again and drank some water from a glass?'

She was far enough away from him now to look into his face.

'That is really good news, Cam,' she added. '*Really* good!'

CHAPTER TEN

THREE DAYS LATER, Maddie was well enough to be transferred to a room on the children's ward. She was kept isolated as her specialists wanted to ensure she stayed quiet, and she remained in bed for most of the day, still sleeping a lot.

A CT scan had revealed that the swelling in her brain had reduced to near normal, but the damaged area needed time—probably weeks—to heal completely.

'We should be able to take her home in a couple of days,' Cam told Lauren, when she arrived to do a late-afternoon shift with the little girl.

'That's great,' Lauren said, wondering just who 'we' was. She hadn't seen Cam since the night she'd stayed with Maddie, and had no idea whether or not the actress was still around.

But the kiss Cam gave her before he left told her she shouldn't be worried. Which she wasn't, really—because he *was* too young for her, and he *would* surely be better off getting back with his wife.

And if that thought made her heart hurt—well, that was just bad luck.

Madge came at midnight and insisted on staying the night.

'I've been sleeping better in that comfortable recliner than in the hotel bed,' she said. 'I'd have been in earlier, but Cam and I went out to dinner—he wanted to talk about Kate. Why he didn't divorce her when she first left him, I'll never know. Now she's found out about the wildlife sanctuary and wants to come back to him.'

Madge paused, and Lauren held her breath.

'Apparently, saving the planet is her new thing, and she can see herself as the actress who gave it all up to save Australia's native animals. Cam's told her the sanctuary has nothing to do with him, it's just on his land, but it seems that's good enough for her.'

Madge looked at Lauren in a helpless way.

'Some people make a mess of their lives, don't they?' she said, so plaintively that Lauren had to give her a hug.

'It'll all work out,' she said. 'And won't Maddie like having her mother around?'

'Hmph!' said Madge. 'As if that woman's ever been a mother—not in the real sense of the word. She got pregnant so she could marry

Cam, and as soon as Maddie arrived she virtually handed her over to me to raise—well, me and Cam. She'd found religion at that stage and was working with church youth groups, putting on strange so-called religious plays. "Street theatre", they called it. Load of old rubbish! Cam was working in a bar at night and trying to get to lectures and study by day, as well as help me with Maddie. The house was full of placards that said *All for God*—which I didn't disagree with at all. But I did think God would probably have preferred her to be a mother—for a little while at least.'

Lauren had to smile. She could imagine how much work a new baby could be, and she wondered just what Madge had had to give up to help Cam raise his daughter.

'What had you been doing before?' she asked.

Madge smiled. 'Running a very successful legal aid business. Most of my clients were single mothers…many trying to get away from abusive husbands.' She looked ruefully at Lauren, then added, 'For a while I thought I could do it all—mind Maddie and work from home, all that stuff—but the reality was very different, and I soon knew I wasn't doing either job particularly well.'

'Oh, Madge, what a loss for you—a career like that!'

Madge smiled again. 'Not such a loss when the reward was a beautiful granddaughter who needed me and a son who needed back-up so he could get his life back together again.'

They sat in silence for a while.

Then Madge said, 'Get off home with you and get some sleep. You have to look after yourself as well as all of us, you know.'

Lauren grinned at her. 'My presence is purely selfish—it's years since I read the Pooh books.'

'Out!' Madge said, but she smiled.

Although something in that smile told Lauren she was worried, and now that Maddie was getting better, there was only Cam left for Madge to worry about. Was she concerned that Kate, if she came back into their lives, would hurt him again?

The thought brought silly tears to Lauren's eyes and an aching tightness to her throat. Knowing he was too young for her didn't stop her loving him, and she couldn't bear the thought of him being hurt.

It was a couple of days before Lauren was free to get up to the hospital to see Maddie again, because the cat had had kittens and the dog had turned cat-protector, not allowing anyone near them—which meant that when her long-suffering cleaner needed to clean the back of the house Lauren had to take Henry for a long walk.

As he knew she was the source of food for himself *and* the cat, Henry had allowed her close enough to check each tiny animal, and today, with the kittens' eyes now open, and their adventures taking them further from their mother, she couldn't resist picking up the little pure black male and tucking him inside her jacket while she and Henry walked.

When she took the kitten back, it was accepted by the others as if it had never been away. Which was why, when the day came for her to go to the hospital—possibly for the last time, she once again kidnapped—or catnapped—the little black one and took it with her.

Cam was there, and her heart flipped at the sight of him, but the smile he offered her in greeting was wan, and something about the way he stood by the bed told her to stay clear.

Kate?

Was he back with her?

It's for the best, her head muttered at her, but her heart would have none of it. All she wanted to do was hold him—try to ease away the strain she could see in every sinew of his body.

Her body tensed…until she realised she might squash the kitten! And that thought turned her attention to Maddie, who was overjoyed as the tiny creature tumbled over her in the hospital bed, and snuggled up in her small hands.

'I *have* to go home, Daddy, so I can see them all,' she announced—which was when Kate walked in.

'You've brought an *animal* in here?' she said to Lauren, anger burning in her eyes. 'Into a *hospital*?

Lauren was taken aback by this virtual stranger being so upset. Was it because she was Maddie's mother?

'I thought it might cheer Maddie up—she's been waiting and waiting for the kittens to be born.'

'And she probably got the virus from the cat!' Kate stormed, lifting the kitten off the bed and pushing it none-too-gently into Lauren's hands.

'There are eight,' Lauren said, ignoring the other woman and turning to Maddie, 'and you can come and see them all when you get home.'

'Only when she's well enough to be up and about,' Kate said.

Lauren's stomach tightened. So Madge's fears that Kate wanted to come back into their lives had been right. The woman was obviously taking over from Madge as Maddie's carer as carelessly and thoughtlessly as she'd left her child in the first place.

Lauren walked away from them. It was more

than she could bear to think about Kate upsetting Maddie and Madge with her behaviour. Moving into the house—into Cam's bed?—and then, as the limited social life at the Lakes struck her, walking away again. Hurting all of them—hurting Cam.

No wonder he looked so strained.

Although maybe Kate would find Cam and Maddie were all she needed for her to decide to stay on.

Maybe that would be best for all of them.

Because surely then her own feelings for Cam, and the anxiety they caused her, would simply fade away.

Maddie came home the following day, having been prescribed bed rest, with occasional short walks or playing with her toys as exercise.

And that afternoon Maddie's idea of a short walk constituted a visit to Lauren—although Lauren knew full well it was really a visit to the kittens.

Maddie sat quietly on the floor, Henry beside her, and played with all of them. But her hands kept going back to the little black fellow, and Lauren knew, when the time came for the litter to leave its mother, that that particular kitten would become Maddie's.

But Lauren could see the little girl was tiring.

'Come on,' she said. 'I'll drive you home.'

'I don't want to drive. I want to go through the bush. I need to smell the trees again,' Maddie said, with the querulous tones of a child still weak and unwell.

'Then I'll piggyback you home,' Lauren countered, and Maddie agreed with delight.

From the top of the front steps, she clambered onto Lauren's back. 'Daddy says I'm too big for piggybacks now,' Maddie said, her lips close to Lauren's ear.

'Daddy's right,' Lauren told her as she took up the solid weight and began to trudge towards what she still thought of as Henry's house.

They must have just passed the halfway mark, and Lauren was flagging, when Cam appeared.

'She's far too heavy for you to be carrying her like that,' Cam said, the crossness in his voice betraying the anxiety he had to have been feeling when he'd been told Maddie had wandered off to Lauren's.

'She's all yours,' Lauren said, letting Maddie slide to the ground. 'I did want to drive her, but she wanted to smell the trees.'

'Of course she did,' Cam said, his voice scratchy as he gathered his daughter in his arms. 'I think we all do, don't we, Mads?'

Maddie put her arms around his neck in a hug and smiled at him. 'I saw all the kittens, but the black one is my favourite.'

'Better that than wanting all of them,' Cam murmured to Lauren, his face close enough for her to see the lines of strain on it, and to read a kind of despair in his eyes.

The air between them seemed charged with some kind of force, prickling her skin with heat, yet sliding icy fingers down her spine. She wanted to hold him, tell him she loved him, but knew that would make things worse.

She touched his cheek, unable not to, and said, 'You'll be all right...' as casually as she could. Because right now he looked as if nothing would ever be right for him again.

Lauren hurried home, trying not to think about what was happening at his place—refusing to think about where Kate might be sleeping.

Plenty of bedrooms, she told herself, *not that it's any of your business.*

None at all.

Apart from Maddie coming to visit and play with the kittens, and Kate cooing over the animals when Lauren was on shift at the sanctuary, Lauren had seen little of her neighbours.

After that first visit, Madge always drove

Maddie over to play, and usually went on into the village to get a few groceries before returning to collect her granddaughter. One day her return coincided with the end of Lauren's morning session.

'Let her play a little longer and come and have a cup of tea with me,' she said to Madge, who accepted with alacrity.

'Anything to keep me away from that woman,' Lauren heard her mutter as they walked through to the big kitchen.

'Madge is staying for a cuppa,' Lauren called through to the laundry.

'So I can stay longer?' Maddie replied, with utter delight in her voice.

But as they sat at the huge old kitchen table Lauren could see from Madge's face that all was not well.

'Maddie's fine,' she told her, pouring Madge a cup of tea and pushing a plate of warm scones towards her.

'It's not Maddie I'm worried about,' Madge said, then bit her lip. 'I promised myself I wouldn't talk about it,' she added, looking so upset that Lauren wanted to hug her.

'Then don't,' she said. 'Just sit and relax, have your tea, and there's jam and cream for the scones. There's something I want to ask you about anyway. Last night at the Regional Fire Service meeting they were talking about getting someone in to do the books and fill in all the government paperwork. I wondered if you might be interested.'

She paused, looking at Madge.

'The RFS is a volunteer organisation,' she added, 'and we get plenty of younger men and women—and quite a few older ones too—who are keen. They practise hard, give lectures, et cetera. But book work! They seem to have a complete horror of it. But it has to be done and Nellie, whose been doing it for thirty years, really wants out. She's seventy-nine, and she feels she's done enough.'

'Well, I think that would be far more interesting than joining a quilting group or even the bridge club,' Madge said, perking up considerably.

'You could probably do both. Well, the bridge club *and* the RFS—Nellie's a bridge player. Would you like me to take you down to the service base, show you around, and maybe meet up with Nellie so she can explain the job? It's not full-time, and really there are no set hours—although it's always good to go to the meetings so you know what's going on. What do you think?'

'Lead me to it,' Madge said, a huge grin on

her face. 'It's just exactly what I need, and now Maddie's spending most of her time over here, until she goes to school, I've plenty of free time to work out what the job entails.'

She called to Maddie, who left the laundry and came in carrying the black kitten.

'He's not quite old enough to leave his mum,' Lauren said gently. 'But another week and he'll be all yours.'

'But then I'll be at school and he'll have no one to play with,' she said, in such tragic tones that Lauren had to hide a smile.

'Not really,' Lauren said. 'Because the mother cat is really yours too, and she can go home with you when he goes. Debbie is busy finding homes for all the other kittens, so everything will be fine.'

Maddie beamed and flung her arms around Lauren's neck. 'I do love you, Lauren,' she said—just as Cam appeared through the laundry door, a kitten in one hand and a watchful Henry by his side.

Lauren hoped her delight in seeing him wasn't making her glow—that the warmth she felt inside wasn't visible on her face.

'Now the whole family's here,' she said, hoping her voice was light and casual. Although to her it sounded kind of squeaky—a dead giveaway of her excitement.

'Not really,' Madge muttered, glaring at her son. 'Maddie, it's time to go. You need some lunch before you have your rest. Put the kitten back with his mother and meet me at the car.'

She whisked away, tea half-drunk, a jammy, creamy half-scone abandoned on her plate.

Was she upset about Kate taking over what had been her place in their lives since Maddie's birth? Or with Cam for allowing it?

Cam was looking equally bemused by his mother's abrupt departure, but rather then get involved with the family dynamic, Lauren told him about their conversation.

'I've been talking to Madge about doing some voluntary bookwork for the Regional Fire Service,' she said, as casually as she could to the man still standing in her kitchen with a kitten in one hand.

It was so good to see him, right there in front of her, and every atom in her being wanted to get up and walk over to him and hold him in her arms—kitten and all.

But the ghost of Kate hovered between them.

And, as if she'd conjured the woman up, Cam spoke her name.

'I've asked Kate—again—to sign the divorce papers,' he said, forcing his hands not to clench because of the kitten in one of them. 'I sent her the papers over a year ago, and gave her another set when she came here. Now I've told her I want them signed before she goes.'

He watched Lauren study him for a moment.

'Goes? Don't you feel you should give it some time?' she asked quietly, absentmindedly pushing half a scone around her plate—not looking at him. 'I mean, with Maddie being so sick, and things only just getting back to normal, shouldn't you at least try to see if it could work—for all your sakes?'

'Not for mine,' he said savagely. 'Nor Maddie's. Kate's barely spent ten minutes with her since she's been here, but she's seen the house, and the sanctuary, and now she pictures herself as Lady Bountiful, lording it over the locals, having fundraising parties with any celebrities she can find and generally settling in.' He paused, before adding, 'She acts all the time—seeing herself in different scenarios and playing out different parts with no thought for anyone else.'

'So what are you going to do?' Lauren asked,

And Cam realised that was really what he'd come to her to ask, and he felt ashamed. Lauren was more to him than someone he went to for help, someone he'd trusted to sit with Maddie while he slept.

Lauren was his life, his future, but what could he offer her? Not even marriage, the way things were.

He turned around, gave the kitten back to its mother, scratched Henry's ears and then slipped out through the back door, his arms aching with the longing to hold Lauren to him, his body aching to have her body pressed to his.

He'd walked over to give himself some breathing space—to smell the trees, as Maddie had said—but really to clear his mind of Kate's incessant chatter about how 'we' could do this, and 'we' could do that—all the time talking about the house and using the plural 'we', as though their marriage was already mended, in spite of their sleeping in different rooms, and his pleas that she sign the divorce papers.

'You're only just back in time,' Debbie chided him when he returned. 'Local radio wants a chat with you—they're phoning in a few minutes.'

'What do they want to chat about?' Cam demanded, not really in the mood for putting on a performance—although he had to admit Debbie's efforts on his behalf had increased the number of people seeking his help with their various animals. Business was beginning to look good.

'It's not an "on air" chat. It's what Lauren was talking to you about—you doing a regular question-and-answer thing. They can set it up so you can do it from home…or really wherever you are. Think how thrilled people would be if you stopped preg-testing a sheep, or something, to chat about their budgie!'

Debbie picked up the receiver on the ringing phone.

'It's them,' she said. 'Go through to your office and I'll put it through there.'

Helplessly resigning himself to the force that was Debbie, he went through to his office.

Lauren had an afternoon shift at the sanctuary and, well aware she'd be as welcome as smallpox if she ran into Kate, she slipped in through the side gate. Helen was there, drawing up the roster for the next few weeks, frowning over the usually simple procedure.

'Trouble?' Lauren asked.

Helen uttered a few pithy swear words.

'It's that woman,' she said in arctic tones when she looked up from her work. 'Fair enough, Beth's left—she was always going to stop about this time—but that woman has her absolutely terrified about childbirth, undoing all the good work in the antenatal classes Beth's been going to. Claims she was hospitalised for months after Maddie's birth, but Madge tells me she was offered a job in a play and took it—three days after she brought Maddie home.'

'This is Kate you're talking about.'

'Who else?' Helen demanded. 'And even though Beth's fairly level-headed she can't help thinking about the things Kate told her. And then there's this idea she's got that we should be on the tourist map, with people coming in to cuddle the animals. Ever tried explaining the word "sanctuary" to an airhead? Because that's what she is—a dangerous airhead. How someone as kind and understanding as Cam ever came to marry her beats me.'

'Well, if you can fit them between my working hours, I'd be happy to do extra shifts, and I can easily come over in the evening to do night feeds and lock up.'

Helen sighed. 'I know you would—I'm happy to do more myself—but we started this, your father and Henry and me, as a community project that everyone could be part of, and *she's* disrupting it—popping in to grab an animal that doesn't know her for a photo shoot. Wanting signs put up for tourists. That kind of thing… People won't have it,' Helen said, and Lauren understood.

The locals were proud of their sanctuary, and did whatever they could to help. But to turn it into a commercial venture—of course they'd buck at that.

'Can you talk to Cam?' Helen asked.

Lauren shrugged. From what she'd seen, Kate

took little notice of anyone else's ideas or opinions—probably least of all Cam's.

The man himself appeared at that moment.

'Debbie's talked the local radio station into giving me a talk-back session once a week,' he said, in such morose tones that both women laughed.

'It will be good for business,' Helen told him, 'and Henry did it—how hard can it be?'

'I'm more worried about sounding pathetic than having any difficulty with it.'

'You could never sound pathetic,' Helen assured him. 'Did you want something?'

'Sane company?' he said hopefully, and they laughed again. 'Actually, I saw Lauren sneaking into the sanctuary and I wanted her to look at some drone pictures I've been taking. I'm not certain I've got the knack yet. Can you spare her?'

Helen smiled at him. 'I can if you put in a plug for some volunteers for the sanctuary on your first broadcast,' she said, and Lauren was glad she didn't blame him for his wife chasing so many away.

CHAPTER ELEVEN

CAM LED THE WAY—not back into his rooms, but out to the shed, where he proudly displayed a drone, sitting on a table by a computer monitor.

'I found Henry's drone and fixed it up, and I've been practising with it. I've flown it over the burnt-out bush, checking for any wildlife, but apart from a couple of wallabies in the regrowth beneath the trees there's not much.'

'You've done well to get the pictures as clear as they are.'

'I've had plenty of spare time,' he said, and the hoarseness in his voice told her more than the words.

She leaned closer as she flicked through the images, stopping at one that was less clear. He caught her hand and helped direct it to another shot in the corner of the screen. His fingers tightened on hers, spirals of desire swirling through her at his touch.

Then they were gone, as he released her hand

and tapped the picture in the corner, enlarging it to show the distinctive diamond shapes on the skin of a large snake. She knew it was a python of some kind.

Cam straightened up and stepped aside so she could study what he'd found. He moved a little distance from her, facing the front of the shed.

'It's killing me…this,' he said. 'Not being able to see you properly, to sit and talk with you—'

'Of course you can—we're friends, remember? And that's what friends do. Not too much, though, while you're trying to make a go of your marriage.'

'Marriage!' he snorted. 'It's hardly that.' He paused, before adding in a voice that had a hint of a tremor in it, 'It's Maddie, you see. I just can't let Kate take the divorce to court when there's even the slightest chance of her getting custody. You've seen enough of Kate to know what Maddie's life would be like.'

'Oh, Cam…' Lauren sighed as she spoke, then stood up and slipped her arms around him from behind, clasping her hands around his waist, pressing her body against his in a friendly *there-there* kind of hug.

They both turned towards the door now, and Lauren peered over Cam's shoulder, aware that he'd been looking out for Kate all along. And totally aware of the loss he dreaded.

The big black saloon that drove up caught both of them by surprise.

A smallish, very well-dressed man got out and strode towards the house.

'Is he from the radio station, do you know?' Cam asked.

Lauren, after a final hug, let go of him and came to stand beside him. 'He's not a local, I'm sure. Unless he's a fairly new arrival,' she said.

Cam shook his head. 'He doesn't look like a lakesider to me. Anyway, Debbie knows I'm here if I'm needed. Let's get back to the snake—do you know what it is?'

He sat down in front of the computer and Lauren stood behind him, not touching him, although she was aware of every line of his body, every breath he took…

They heard the visitor coming before he reached the shed, and his, 'Good afternoon,' came to them from the door.

'What is it you're looking at?' he asked, crossing to where they were, peering at the screen. 'Python of some kind from the look of it,' the man said. 'Harmless, of course, but nice to see one in the burnt-out area. Shows good regeneration.'

He straightened up.

'I'm Russell Blair, by the way,' he said, looking at Cam, 'and I've got your divorce papers here. Kate's signed them and I've witnessed them, along with that lass from your office.'

He handed the papers to Cam, who looked from the papers to the man in disbelief.

'She's packing now—Kate. I'm sorry I wasn't in the country when your little girl got sick. I'd have come down with Kate and fixed up the paperwork then. I'm going to marry her, you see. It's just that she likes the drama—stringing me along, dashing off on the slightest excuse, trying out different roles she might fancy living... But you probably know that! Anyway, it's all settled now.'

He turned from Cam, glanced at Lauren, then looked back at Cam.

'I guess you'll be glad to have it done with.'

Lauren could feel the heat climbing into her cheeks, so she fiddled with the picture on the computer, not sure that she could identify one python from another.

Cam followed Russell Blair back to his car, where Kate, with Debbie's help, was installing what seemed like masses of luggage into the boot.

'Never one to travel light,' Russell remarked, but he made no move to help.

Cam walked around the vehicle to where his

wife stood at the open front door. 'Did you tell Maddie you were going?' he asked.

Kate shook her head. 'She won't care,' she said. 'She doesn't know me at all. No one really does—except for Russell.'

Well, good luck to him, Cam thought. *I've never had a clue.* And not to say goodbye to Maddie showed how little she cared about the child she'd brought into the world.

Lauren had remained in the shed, although she came to the door as the car drove off.

Cam turned towards her, face alight with joy. '*Now* we can get married!' he said, excitement filling his body.

But the woman in the doorway shook her head.

'It was never Kate or your marriage stopping us, Cam,' she said softly—and, he thought, sadly. 'Although while you were still married it was impossible...which made it easier to pretend for a bit. But the real problem remains—and that's your age. I'm too old for you. You need someone young and vibrant—someone who can give you sisters or brothers for Maddie—someone to make a family with. You need to get out and meet people, go to the pub...whatever. Get a life outside your work—for Maddie's sake as well as your own.'

She reached out, took his hand, and looked into his eyes.

'Don't make it hard for me, Cam,' she said.

And then he saw the pain she'd hidden in her practical words, only too evident in her eyes.

She slipped away through the scrub that stood between their houses, somehow making a wall of it—a no-man's-land—and cutting herself off from him.

He'd give her time to get home and then phone her, he thought, certain she wasn't really at all convinced that whatever it was between them couldn't…wouldn't…*shouldn't* continue.

But Lauren wasn't available.

She was working hard, Janet told him when he tried to phone her. She had a lot of lost time to make up with her paperwork and accounting. And a big meeting for the Regional Fire Service was approaching, and she was secretary of that. Such a lot to do…

Janet made it all sound utterly reasonable— even mostly true—so he could hardly go crashing over there.

Except…

Wasn't Madge talking about joining the RFS—hadn't there been talk of her doing the book work?

He'd get Debbie to babysit Maddie and take Madge to the meeting himself.

He sat down at the computer to check when and where the meeting was to be held. He wasn't giving up just yet.

Lauren hadn't been lying when she'd said she had a lot to do. The end of the financial year *was* coming up, and all her income and expenditure had to be made ready for her accountant.

Plus, there was the RFS stuff. And the work *that* would involve this year was going to be mammoth, as all the donations they'd received in the aftermath of the bush fires had to be listed, and then another list made of what these generous gifts—even the smallest ones—had been put towards.

And on top of that the members had to discuss a new way forward—start thinking of a plan to be better prepared than they had been. She knew one of the main projects had to be finding a way to improve communication. Not just between the different fire services, but between them and the people on outlying properties, who relied solely on the radio or their telephones—on power being connected, when often it was the first service lost.

All this busy thinking had brought her home, the scents of the scrub passing unnoticed. But she knew all her thoughts had, in part, been a way of avoiding thinking of Cam completely—

just for a little while…or perhaps a bit longer than a little while…hoping avoidance would help her accept that this was how it should be.

And if even contemplating a future of seeing less of Cam caused a deep, physical ache, then she'd just have to learn to live with it.

You have to think ahead, in situations like this, she told herself as she headed upstairs to shower and change for her evening clinic.

Her at sixty when he'd be in the prime of life at fifty. Not that sixty was old…but the age difference would be more marked—especially if she did develop dementia…

Standing in the shower, warm water cascading over her, she let her thoughts continue to run riot.

All Cam-based.

It had been not just lust—she hoped—but probably also a need for closeness with a woman that had made her appealing to him. After all, she'd been there, and available, hadn't she?

But rationalising all this—and what had happened between them—didn't make her heart any less sore, or the pain of love any less overwhelming.

Not that he'd ever know.

No word of love had ever passed between them.

She was keeping the sudden revelation of her feelings to herself, while as for Cam—from their first meeting he'd been obsessed with marriage, which was probably what he needed from a practical point of view. He could hardly expect his mother to go on taking care of his household for ever.

Enough! Get dry, get dressed, concentrate on her patients, then get on with work for the RFS.

She had to find out if they could use some of the donations they'd received to put overhead powerlines underground. At the height of the fires they'd had thousands of people without power for weeks, and it hadn't been good enough.

Her session was busy, and she was late making her way back to the sanctuary, where she was on the late shift.

She snuck in through the outside gate—she could do this. Carry on as usual, get back into her old routines—her old life.

And if her heart ached with the pain of something that could never be… Well, that was for her to know—not others—and definitely not Cam.

Cam had watched her go, had heard the note of finality in her words, and thought maybe she was right—although he did wonder if she just plain didn't love him, but hadn't wanted to hurt him by saying so.

He decided it was useless to keep thinking

about it and went off to see what the tireless Debbie had thought up for him now.

'We could sell products,' she announced as he went in. 'Special dog and cat food, and seeds that attract native birds. Just as an extra...you know. And I've had an email from a young man whose budgie isn't very well. It's on a self-feeder and he thinks it might be eating too much. That would be a good first question for your column.'

'My column?' he said feebly as he watched her packing up, ready to leave as soon as her ever-reliable Harry turned up.

'For the paper,' she said. 'They want it Monday. There's a note on your desk about who to email it to and the number of words, et cetera. The paper comes out on Thursday, you see.'

He thanked her and went into his office-cum-consulting room. There must be six little memos there—including the details of his 'column'. But being busy would be good.

He could hear Maddie and Madge, talking in the kitchen. He'd go and join them, maybe have a beer, and look into what kind of things could go wrong with budgerigars later.

Maddie was parading in her school uniform—having been pronounced ready to return to school on Monday by her doctors. She and Madge had gone into the village to get it earlier and had obviously made a day of it, as new shoes and a sensible wide-brimmed hat were included in their purchases.

'We can't go into the playground without a hat,' Maddie told him. 'It's a rule!'

'And a good one,' he agreed.

But when she suggested she go over to Lauren's, to show her the new uniform, Cam said it was a bit late and maybe Helen and the wombats would like to see it instead.

She skipped happily off, and he poured a glass of wine for his mother and sat down at the kitchen table.

'Were you here when Kate left?' he asked, and she shook her head.

'Although we did run into them in the village,' Madge explained. 'I really do not understand that woman—never have,' she continued. 'She was far more interested in introducing me to her fancy man in his fancy car than in saying goodbye to her daughter. Although I must admit Maddie showed little interest in either of them, just standing in front of the shop window trying her new hat at different angles.'

'Do you think Maddie realises Kate's gone for good this time?' Cam asked.

Madge sighed. 'Really, Cam, I don't think she's ever felt any connection. I doubt she has ever seen Kate as her mother—more as some exotic being who drifted into her life when she was still in the haze of her illness. She certainly hasn't any childhood memories of her. She was barely two when Kate left.'

'Well, I hope that's the end of it,' Cam said, suddenly realising he was right back where he'd started when he'd arrived in Australia—in a big old house with his mother and daughter.

Well, there was the sanctuary. And Debbie. But Lauren had been right. He had to get involved with the local community, if only to distract his thoughts from Lauren herself...

But why? He didn't *want* to distract himself from thoughts of Lauren—not a bit of it. She was the best thing that had happened to him in his entire life—including being given his own vet practice and building his own ultralight.

And he loved her.

Had he told her that?

He'd certainly told her he was smitten—but that might not have been taken as love...

And he'd certainly mentioned marriage—but had he officially proposed?

Of course not. He hadn't been able to until today, when the divorce papers had been signed.

He'd do it now—go and ask her. She was in the sanctuary. He'd seen her walk around the side of the house.

And then somehow Madge and Maddie and

Debbie were all there too—going into the sanctuary.

School uniform showing off time?

He pushed ahead of them.

CHAPTER TWELVE

LAUREN WAS HELPING Helen check the stock in the sanctuary when Madge, Maddie and Cam came in through the house door, Debbie trailing behind them.

Her heart, for all she knew it shouldn't, flipped at the sight of the man she loved—loved to distraction, really.

Although how she—an intelligent, rational, not-so-young woman—had allowed herself to fall in love with a younger man, she didn't know.

Nor did she really know where things would go from here.

Or why there were suddenly all these people here…

Cam stepped away from his entourage, and would have taken her hand if she hadn't backed away.

But, seemingly unperturbed, he took his stance in front of her and spoke with calm authority.

'Lauren, I love you. Will you do me the honour of marrying me?' he asked.

You are not going to faint, Lauren said sternly to herself, clutching the desk in the sanctuary while her knees turned to jelly. *You don't do fainting.*

'Please say yes, Lauren!' Maddie said, squeezing forward to stand close to her friend and frowning. 'You look sick, like I did when I was in hospital, and not at all happy.'

'She's happy inside,' Cam said, looking serenely composed but probably inwardly laughing at the position he'd put her in—the wretch. 'Not right away, of course,' he continued, bland as milk. 'But in a few months—once we've had a chance to work things out...like which house we want to live in—'

'Lauren's!' Maddie said, clapping with delight. 'Because Henry and Puss the cat live there, and there's a little room that looks out over the lake that Lauren said I could sleep in whenever I came to stay. She used to sleep in it when she was little.'

Lauren continued to grip the desk and closed her eyes. She had a four-year-old—no, a four-and-a-half-year-old—organising her future.

'Lauren?' Madge said, her voice soft...anxious.

Lauren opened her eyes and smiled weakly

at Madge. 'I'm fine,' she managed, and at the words her fighting spirit returned. 'Although whether your son will be when I finish with him over this nonsense, I can't say.'

'But *is* it nonsense?' Madge asked.

Lauren shook her head.

'Daddy just didn't do it right,' Maddie explained to her grandmother. 'He should have got down on one knee and given her a ring.'

Lauren shook her head again. This family had her beat!

'Daddy will do all that part when he's somewhere private,' Cam told his small relationship advisor.

'Can I watch?' Maddie asked.

But Cam's words had been weak, and Lauren realised just what a strain this must be for him.

'We'll talk about it later,' she promised Maddie, as Madge began herding the child and Debbie towards the door.

Lauren walked with them, thinking to escape but knowing she needed to talk to Cam.

Talk?

More like yell and shout and throw a tantrum, if she could remember how to do it from her two-year-old days.

Madge stopping her with a soft hand on her arm.

'He shouldn't have put you on the spot like

that, but it would make me very happy if you did decide to marry him,' she said. 'Me *and* Maddie. And not just for dogs or cats or rooms, but because you make him happy.'

She gave Lauren a peck on the cheek and left, with Maddie talking excitedly about her new room.

'I'm off too,' Helen said, her arms raised in the air, as if well aware that a lot more had to be said.

Lauren turned to look at the man who remained, smiling genially—if a little anxiously.

'What have you done?' she muttered.

He held out his hand. She put hers into it and he clasped it tightly, pulling her closer until he could put his lips to hers in a kiss that said far more than words.

Oh, if it could only be, she thought as she leant into him, feeling the solidity of his support and her overwhelming sense of love.

He eased her a little away, so he could look into her eyes, but kept her hands captive in his.

'I know all your arguments about the difference in our ages and they're rubbish. Older men marry younger women all the time. And as for family—if you'd like children…well, you're still young enough. Lots of women in their forties are having children these days.'

Stunned by all that had happened, she could only stare at him.

'And as for your biggest fear, my darling...' He looked deep into her eyes. 'I know we've never spoken of it, but it's your father's illness, isn't it? Your over-active imagination has you declining into some form of dementia and me having to look after you. You've been there and done that, and you know how hard it was, but the doctor in you must know it's not hereditary, even though some things that could lead to it are genetic.'

'It's a lottery,' she mumbled, and he drew her close again.

'So shall I tell you something?' he whispered in her ear. 'The love we share will give us many happy years, and I would willingly care for you. You didn't stop loving your father, and I have no intention of ever—*ever*—stopping loving you. You are my friend—my mate, in Aussie terms— my lover and hopefully my wife, and I will love you for ever and a day.'

He drew her close again, and his kiss told her all the things he'd said and many, many more.

The cloud of fear disappeared, and she knew the love she felt for him must be shining in her eyes.

'Do I need to officially say yes?' she asked,

aware that her answer was already given as she pressed her lips to his.

'You just have to say, *I love you, Cam*,' he said. 'Because you do, don't you?'

She stepped back, her hands holding his, and looked into those blue eyes she'd first seen in a dry gully not so very long ago.

'I love you, Cam, more than you could ever imagine.'

And she let him pull her close again and hold her as she knew he would—now and for ever!

They were married by the lake, their friends around them—Maddie clutching the black kitten and the cat, Henry the dog, who'd refused to go and live with anyone else, staunch by Lauren's side.

'It's a wonder someone didn't bring out the wombats and a koala,' Cam said, as he held his wife in his arms and they looked out over the magic of the lake that had led them to love.

'No, but there *is* a drone,' Lauren told him.

And they both looked up so the little drone from the local paper could record this special event.

And smiled.

* * * * *

*If you enjoyed this story, check out
these other great reads from
Meredith Webber*

One Night to Forever Family
Conveniently Wed in Paradise
The Doctors' Christmas Reunion
A Wife for the Surgeon Sheikh

All available now!